Sinful HANDS

PART ONE

USA TODAY BESTSELLING AUTHOR
T.L. SMITH

D1556660

Cover – RBA Design
Photographer – miguelanxo
Editor – Swish Design – Ink Machine Editing – Nice Girl,
Naught Edits
Proofreader – Cruel Ink Editing
Model - Sergio
Formatting – Erica Alexander – Serendipity Formats

BLURB

Lucas
I was obsessed from the beginning.
And once I have an obsession.
It's best you don't get in my way.

Chanel
I tried to stay away.
He was the one who was whispered about on the streets.
The viper that, once he had a taste, would hunt you down and collect you.
And Lucas liked to collect things.
One of those things was me.

The City's Bad Boy

You've missed me, haven't you?
I certainly have missed you all.
But first, before we dive into everything else, have you seen our notorious, always-up-to-no-good, sinful-as-sin Lucas Rossi?
Cousin to the one and only king of the underworld, Keir Rossi.
But do we know much about Lucas other than he can look at any woman and make her question whatever relationship she is in?
Sources say he likes to do the dirty work.
That there is no other like him.
I guess it's time we did some digging.
What do you say, readers?

*W*ith my back arched, and my knees bent, I wonder if I should stretch.

Is that what people do? Fuck what people do.

"We need to talk about this." Keir's voice is right behind me, but my eyes aren't focused on him.

"About what?"

"Don't play coy with me, Lucas." A smirk stretches my lips, but he can't see from where he's standing. "What the fuck are you doing?"

"I guess you'll never know."

"Oh, I know! We all fucking know, Lucas." I hear him take a breath, but I stay where I am. "They are not toys." I look back over my shoulder at him—he appears so large, towering over me. And he is, but I merely smile up at him, showing my teeth at his insistence.

1

"It's best you be on your way, boss."

"Fucking hell, Lucas. One day a woman is going to knock you on your ass and I'm gonna pay her to do it." He stalks off, shaking his head, leaving me there crouched and wondering…

When is the perfect time?

Is it now?

Or should I wait?

I like the anticipation of waiting.

But let's be honest, I am far from a patient man.

"Lucas." I stand, slowly, turning back to see Keir getting in the car. "Behave." Then he is gone.

Behave?

There's no such thing.

Making my way into the bar and brushing off the dirt from my knees, I smile at the person my eyes are set on. *What a pretty little bird.*

I stride right over to her, and her eyes go wide, before offering me a small smile.

"Lucas."

"Mmm." She looks behind her to her friends, who glance the other way.

"I didn't expect to see you so soon."

"Yes, about that. Let's go." I nod toward the door, and she waves goodbye to her friends.

You see, I've had a taste of this one before.

But the smell has changed.

This one though, she was my therapist.

Maybe she shouldn't have mixed business with pleasure.

"How are you, Lucas?" she asks as we get outside.

I keep walking down the alley, not adjusting my pace for her heels, and she follows behind, not questioning where we're going.

"Why don't you ask what you really want to, Sarah?" I turn back to see her put a piece of hair behind her ear.

"You've been staying away. You have missed vital appointments, Lucas. You need help. You know this."

"I thought that's what you were doing when you spread your legs for me, Sarah. Helping." I let the last word tumble from my lips. The river is coming into view as we walk out of the alley and onto the side of the street.

"I was helping. We could have gotten somewhere, Lucas. You have a problem, and the more you work on it, the more maintainable it can be."

"And what exactly *is* my issue?" The water is next to me now, but she keeps her distance. I reach out and pull her close. Her eyes glance at the water before they fall back to me.

I run my hand along her curvy edges—I like that she has something to grip onto. But it's not enough to keep me hooked.

It's… the way she smells.

It has changed.

"Lucas, should we make a time for you to come back?" Her voice is shaky because she's nervous.

She should be.

The back of my hand touches her face, and I stroke down. Her crystal-clear blue eyes watch me.

"I don't think that's gonna work any longer," I tell her, dropping my hand lower until it goes over the curve of her breast. She sucks in a breath, but I keep on dropping lower and lower.

"Why not?" She shakes her head as her lips press together.

My fingers meet the edge of her dress, and I slide it up until I get to her panties, which are already wet.

"Are you excited to see me, Doctor?"

"Lucas." Her voice comes off raspy when we both know she's trying to stay still.

"Yes, Doctor?" I push her panties to the side and insert a finger. It slides in easily, and her hand lifts to touch my shoulder.

"We shouldn't," she says the words but leans into my touch, as I add another finger effortlessly.

"But we are, Doctor." My fingers slide in and out while my thumb applies pressure to her clit. Her forehead lays on my chest while my fingers work their magic. I feel her tightening around me, and as she does, I pull them free. She groans, lifts her head, and looks at me with narrowed eyes.

"That's unfair," she mutters, her voice strained.

I smile and push my fingers back in, two of them, with my thumb circling her clit. She is ready for me, and she can feel it too as her other hand moves to my wrist to try to get me to keep going. To not move as she's coming. "Don't stop, Lucas. I don't want you to stop this time." She's talking about how I used to fuck her.

"But remember how hard you would come, Doctor… all over my hand." There's no other part of me touching her apart from my hand in her pussy. Her hands, though, are all over me.

"Not this time. Don't tease me this time," she almost begs, her hands gripping my jacket and legs trembling as she gets closer.

"Okay, only this time."

Sarah sighs, and her head lolls back to my chest while I pump my fingers in and out of her. When I feel her tightening around my fingers, I use my other hand to push her chest back. "Watch me, Doctor." Her crystal-clear eyes link to mine. "You thought you could be the one to cure me, to make me better, didn't you?" I pause my fingers when she doesn't answer.

She whimpers.

"Answer me."

"Yes, Daddy," she replies, bringing a smile to

my face. My fingers begin moving again, curling to brush that spot which will push her over the final edge.

"You can't fix me, dear. I'm already amazing."

It's then she sees the real me, even in the midst of coming.

My free hand now holds a knife.

"It's impossible to fix something already perfect, Doctor." Then, ever so lightly as she comes, the knife slides across her throat while my hand continues to fuck her. Her moan is interrupted when she chokes on the blood quickly cascading down her chest, her eyes never leaving mine as they grow wider with shock. "See, perfect."

I pull my fingers free and feel my smile spreading as she tries to move away with her hand now firmly grasping her throat. "And you thought you could try to pass on my notes to the police. How stupid do you think I am?"

I step closer as she takes another step back, her hands on her wound trying to stem the blood flow as the river streams behind her.

There is no escaping.

"You were fun, though. I learned so much about myself." I wink, huffing a laugh. "But all good things must come to an end. Goodbye, Doctor." I give her shoulder a gentle push.

Both of her hands leave her neck, as she tries to grab me to stop from falling in, but I step aside and watch. Her mouth opens to release a pointless, garbled scream as she stumbles and plunges into the murky depths of the water below.

Wiping my hands on my trousers, I take one last look at her disappearing form, then leave.

Goodbye, Doctor. It was fun while it lasted.

It always is until they no longer interest me.

*H*e grunts— I hate him.

Grunt.

Grunt.

Grunt.

Just imagine it.

But he isn't the worst.

He's just… a grunter.

Again, it could be worse.

Tonight isn't a typical bad night, but I'm over it already.

His grubby hands grip my waist, and I instantly want to roll off and tell him he needs to go home and fuck his damn wife. Stop being unfaithful. Go home to his kids and spend the money on them.

But why would I do that?

That would be like *cutting off one's nose to spite one's face*, right?

9

He pays nicely, and I'm a whore. A hooker. A trollop. A prostitute. Whatever they like to call those of us who let men pay us for sex.

The client always takes off his wedding ring, like it's sacred to him. Like this little soirée is meant to be some sort of secret that the ring might give away, but we always know the truth.

Let's face it, it's mostly married men who engage in our services. The ones who want things they are too afraid to ask their partners for but are more than happy to request from us. Probably because they're paying and trust that no matter how much we might think of them as scum, we aren't going to voice it.

And believe me, I've wanted to voice it.

Many, many times.

But then again, I have no right to say shit.

Why even stay married, though?

If you're not happy, just leave.

Not one person in the world is stopping you, except *you*!

I don't ever see marriage in my future. I'm what you'd call 'from the bottom of the barrel.' *Trash.* I know it, and I also know that no respectable man will ever want me.

And I've come to terms with that.

I'll let you in on a little secret—the respectable men usually stray. Yes, I know, not what you wanted to hear, right? It's not always what you think…or should I say, *who* you think would use our services.

And these so-called 'respectable men' where do they end up, you ask?

In this cheap-ass hotel room telling me all about their wife at home and what she won't do. Some, as I said, like to keep it a secret, but most want to vent out their frustrations.

She doesn't like doggie.

She won't suck my cock.

I want to call her a whore in the bedroom, but I'm afraid she'll take it personally and leave me and *I don't want her to leave me.*

But, hello! So instead, you cheat and fuck other women?

Let's be real in this and not tell lies.

They all lie.

All men lie.

One day, when I meet a man who doesn't lie, I may just marry him—guess that says everything because I doubt there is one out there.

I don't for one minute believe that statement.

In my line of work, they are liars, cheats, and bastards.

Even this asshole, who I am currently sitting on, and not fucking. No, he just wants me to grind on him.

This shit does nothing for me.

And let me tell you, when I was a teenager, I

used to love it. But with someone I don't find attractive, no matter how hard I try to replace the face with some hot celebrity, I can't seem to get into it.

"Fuck yeah, baby, you like how that feels."

"Oh, yeah, baby." The lie slips from my lips so easily. No kidding, I could be an actress.

Mental note—start looking into auditions.

Could I be any more disinterested? Now I'm thinking about impossibilities.

He moves faster, and I know he's almost there.

Men have weird desires, but this one isn't out of the ordinary, so I have it easy tonight because it could be far, far worse.

"Tell me how much you love my cock, you dirty little slut."

See, he's one of those who wants to talk to his wife like this, but is too afraid.

"So much." I pretend to fake cry out in pleasure when really I want to cry out in frustration.

His eyes light up at my believable expression and he bites his lip.

"Let me kiss you." He groans that way men do when they're close, and I totally ignore his command. I watched *Pretty Woman* once, and the no kissing thing kind of stuck. I'm saving that for *the one* that might mean something to me. *Yeah, even that sounds ridiculous to me.*

I pre-warn them all.

They all agree, until they're in the throes of pleasure.

Most will try.

None ever succeed.

If I must give away my body for money, you can guarantee I'm not about to give away my kisses to just anyone.

But as I grow older, I think *the one* is elusive and will be harder and harder to find.

The guy's phone starts ringing. He glances at it, but he's too close now so he won't stop. The cell quiets, then rings again. This time it's a different ring tone, and within seconds, he has me off him and thrown to the side, his cock still hard as he gets up. I stand, brushing my hair to the side, and stare at the wet patch on his jeans.

"Sir," he answers, and his eyes fall to his cock. He takes a moment to fix himself up.

That, for sure, isn't his wife, which I assumed it was. He nods his head a few times and looks back at me. His eyes skim my dress, but he continues listening to whoever is on the other end of the call.

I gather my purse and look back at him.

He holds out the rest of the money to me, and I walk over to take it. When I grip it, he doesn't let go.

"Okay, sir, I'll be right there." He hangs up.

"I take it that isn't your wife." I smile.

"No, but I'm more afraid of him than my wife."

I nod. There's only one man in this city who could evoke that level of fear, and I stay well and truly far away from him.

"You should stay. I'll be back later."

"No can do, big boy." I give him another fake smile. "I have things to do. You know this." They know they have to book time with me. They can't just order me to come back whenever they want. It won't fit in with my schedule.

This isn't a hook-up for my pleasure. This is what they pay for, so it's all about their satisfaction. Believe me, I get nothing from this, *ever*.

"I want to see you again."

I glance down at his ring. *What was his name again?* I can't remember. I choose to not remember their names. It's easier that way, so I pat his chest and hum, "You know what to do, then." I pull the money from his grasp and head toward the door.

"Tell me something."

My feet stop just before the door, and I turn around to face him. He's watching me intently, his round belly hiding under his button-up shirt. "Do you enjoy it, or is it all fake?"

I give him my only answer; the one I give every client—I wink before I walk out. As I leave the room, I hear a soft laugh behind me.

Outside, the sky is black. It may storm tonight, it may not, I can't be sure.

So I call my brother, and he doesn't answer.

Then I call my neighbor, and luckily she does.

"Where is he?"

She's quiet.

"Merci." I say her name.

"Fuck," she responds. "I thought he would be back by now."

"Where is he?" I ask her again. My hands go to the steering wheel of my shit-ass car while waiting for the answer, and I squeeze tight for a moment before sliding my client's money into my purse.

"Don't kill me."

"Merci," I repeat, my patience running thin and showing in my tone.

"He's at Works Bar." My hands slam on the wheel, hard, then I hang up the phone.

I may die tonight.

CHAPTER TWO

CHANEL

I'm going to throttle him. My hands will wrap tight around his throat as I extinguish the living light from his eyes.

He knows better.

We both do.

Fuck.

I am going to kill him.

Dead as a fucking cockroach beneath my feet.

End of discussion.

I want to pull my hair out with each step I take.

Have I not taught him anything?

Does he not listen to me at all?

Why does he have to be like this?

It's not hard to follow a simple instruction, 'stay away from them,' which, clearly, he ignored.

Dead.

Argh.

This is what I'm left with.

Heels clicking with each step I take into the bar, my eyes scan the area.

I shouldn't be here.

This place is not the place for me.

But sometimes a girl has to do things that are necessary—things she may not want to do.

This is one of them.

For sure.

"You aren't meant to be in here, whore." My head swings in the direction of where that voice came from. The bartender's eyeing me up and down, pulling his lips together in disgust as he glares at me.

"Fuck you!"

His gaze swoops over me again, and I know what's got his nose out of joint. A dress with a slit up the side, that if it rode up, you would see everything. Because I'm not wearing underwear.

"Your funeral." The bartender cackles like a stupid witch, going back to what he was previously doing.

Upon taking a deep breath, I turn away from him.

Fuck. Fuck. Fuck.

This is the last place I want to be.

We all know whose place this is.

Who that person is.

And I've warned him, time and time again.

To. Stay. Away.

Yet, I know, I just *know* he's here with every fiber of my being. Plus, his little rat of a friend told Merci.

He could have been lying, but I suspect not.

I walk past a few patrons, straight to the back door where it's forbidden to enter unless you're invited. I've never been invited and don't ever plan to be.

Who the fuck knows what they do back there?

And the stories I hear? Well, most invitees don't come out functioning properly afterward—if you are a woman, that is. The men? Well, they have full rights to everything, don't they?

It's a man's fucking world here.

My hands give a slight tremble as I reach for the door, but I shake it off. Now is not the time to grow weak. Right now, I need everything in me to do this.

Every-damn-thing.

Especially if I am dealing with *him*.

I've seen him around, heard the whispers, but have never, thankfully, had to meet him.

Seems my luck just ran out, and I'm about to meet the most fucked-up man there is.

Lucas Rossi.

My chipped blue nails clench the door handle,

and when I turn to look over my shoulder, the bartender is eyeing me, waiting to see what I do next.

Will I actually push it open?

Or will I stay on this side, where it's safe?

Taking a deep breath, I prepare myself to push it open.

I have to.

It's for him.

I love him.

He's all I have left. Which is why I'm willingly walking into Hell.

My body is locked tight, and I will myself to turn the fucking handle. Just do it. Do it now!

What could be the worst thing to happen? Oh, yeah, I don't get to walk out because, that's it, I'll be dead.

Fuck this!

Turning the knob quickly, I push the door open with a little more force than needed. I'm immediately met with the aroma of stale cigar smoke in a room that's dark and dingy. There are only a few scattered lights that shine down on a table in the center. All eyes of the men sitting at that round table, with cards in their hands, look up to face me.

"You brought us a toy," one of them says.

I ignore the words as my eyes search the room. Looking for *him*. I have to find *him*. When I don't see him, my breath hitches, and I wonder if this was the right move. Then I see my brother walk out of a back room, holding a tray of glasses. His eyes, the same brown as mine, lock on me and he swears.

"You fucking little shit." My brother's face pulls tight as my words are aimed right at him, and he shakes his head. Then, seeming to remember where he is, he looks back to the table and continues on with what he was doing—serving drinks. I stand there shocked that he's proceeding but watch as he sets a drink in front of every man, then bows and backs away when he's finished.

"You should lose the dress," a man with a wicked gleam in his eyes comments, his eyes traveling the length of my body before settling on my face. I hold his stare, unmoving. He smirks at my reaction and shakes his head, looking away.

"You should, though. Otherwise…" He doesn't finish but looks at my brother, who is now standing at the back door, with a tray in hand. I take in the words he just uttered—and those left unsaid—and bite my lip. I've done worse, so taking off my dress would seem so simple, but that's not why I'm here.

"I came for him, and we're leaving." I glare at my brother. "Brody."

He glances down, then places the tray on a table and makes his way over to me.

"Not so fast. His services aren't finished." The

one who said 'otherwise' is the main talker, it seems. He has long hair tied back in a ponytail and a sneer that appears to just sit over his face.

"They are! He's underage," I reply, refusing to be intimidated, pulling my stupid brother closer to me by the sleeve of his dress shirt.

"I'm eighteen in like two weeks," my brother grumbles next to me.

I can't help the scoff that leaves my mouth. "He's leaving." I announce to the room and step back toward the door, my hand gripping my brother's arm with no respite.

"You open that door, I'll put a bullet in your brother's head."

My hand stills over the knob, and the gruff, irate sound of that voice hits me hard.

I know who it is without having to turn around while everyone else goes deathly silent.

I may have never met Lucas, but everyone on the streets knows who he is. You'd be stupid not to know of him.

While he isn't the leader of the mafia—his cousin, Keir, is—Lucas is feared down here even more so than Keir. Keir doesn't usually bother to come to this shitty area where the scum live to play with us. Because, trust me, playing is what he does.

The stories I've heard, the marks I've seen, we all know better than to piss where he eats. Yet, here

I am, walking straight into his bar, like I have not a care in the world.

While Keir stays in the better part of the city and in his nice houses, Lucas is the exact opposite. He will slum it and not give a fuck.

He's the only person in this shitty little neighborhood just out of New York who drives a car worth more than any house you'd find here— probably double the price—yet, no one, and I mean no one, would touch it.

We all know our place.

Though, it seems for family, I've forgotten mine. I glance at my brother.

"You seem to be under the impression you can walk in here and take what you want." He pauses. "*My* things."

"He's my brother," I bite back, and a small hiss leaves someone at my outburst. I can't see him, since he's sitting at the end of the table where no light shines directly above him, but I know he can see me. Every inch of me as I stand under the main light near the door.

"I don't give a fuck if he's your son." Brody tenses next to me. He damn well should be uneasy, making me come down here to get his ass. "Now, do as the man said and lose the dress."

I look over at Brody.

"I'll do it, if he can go."

"You're negotiating with me?" His voice is stern. "Stupid woman."

I hold my ground. Brody knows what I do to make ends meet, but that doesn't mean he has to see it.

"If he goes, I'll do as you want," I repeat, my tone even and agreeable. I can hear the sound of tapping on wood. Squinting, I see one of his hands is on the table, holding cards, while the finger of the other taps repeatedly. A ring he's wearing catches my eye as those strong hands continue to *tap, tap, tap*. I wonder how someone's hands can be so attractive. Because his certainly are.

"You can go, boy."

I open the door, yanking Brody through the opening, then lean in so only he can hear me. "Go straight the fuck home and lock yourself in," I order, shoving him farther and closing the door in his face. The last thing I see is the shock of his gaping mouth, ready to speak, as I slam the door behind him.

When I hear his footsteps moving away, I turn around to accept what's coming next from the men in this room.

He is standing right in front of me when I do. Dressed in a black button-up shirt with black slacks and combat boots. It seems odd to be wearing a pair of scuffed boots with his experienced suit, but he pulls it off.

It's not hard, though, if you look like him. When you first come across Lucas Rossi, you think, *Shit, that man is attractive. How is that even possible?*

The stories about him should make him ugly, hideous, a monster. But he's young, in his late twenties, maybe early thirties, with tanned skin and slight stubble dusting his jaw. He has a tragus piercing in one ear, silky dark hair that's perfectly mussed, and wood-colored eyes. Like the bark on a tree that has all variations of brown variegated through them. They are intense, and as they stare at me, it feels like they're raking through my soul, scratching at it to see what's underneath.

Well, isn't he in for a huge surprise because there's nothing.

I have nothing left.

"You weren't planning on…" he pauses, licks his lips, and my eyes track each movement, "… running, were you?" He leans forward and grips a piece of my dull brown hair and then drops it. Where his is vibrant, mine hasn't been washed for days.

I choose to not speak.

"What did you say your name was?" he pries.

Again, I keep my mouth shut. I watch as the muscle in his neck tics at my non-response. He isn't used to someone not jumping at his every command, and right now I don't give a shit about what he wants.

"Tsk, tsk, tsk." He steps back and looks down over my body. "Remove it."

Instantly, I reach for the hem of my dress, and his eyes track my movements. I slide my hand up my leg, showing my thigh, as I raise the dress higher. After a few blinks, I glance up to see him showing no emotion whatsoever. Then, before I can go any farther, he steps close to me again.

"What do you smell like?" He leans in and, before I have a chance to react, his face is buried in my neck and he's breathing me in.

What the ever-loving fuck?

I feel the warmth of his chest hovering above mine, as his breath tickles my neck, all while I stand there shocked and still. Then he moves his body even closer, and I feel his erection pressed against me.

And do you want to know the worst part?

I like the feel of his body against mine.

He possesses something no one has ever had over me—*power*—and he holds it in the palm of his hand, as if it were a toy.

"Vanilla, musk, with something a little… spicy," he remarks, then pulls back. I watch him lick his lips, his pupils dilated while his eyes roam over me. "My last favorite flavor was cotton candy, but I soon got sick of it."

"What did you do?" I don't know why I asked that question, it just slipped from my mouth. His lips twitch, it seems he's pleased that I asked. And surprised.

"I killed her." He says those three words as if I asked him what he had for dinner. Then he licks his teeth and nods to my dress.

"Now, remove it. Otherwise, you'll end up next to her."

CHAPTER THREE

CHANEL

*T*he stories of Lucas aren't made up. The man is the worst of the worst. And doing what I do for work, I know this. The girls all know him, or of him. *Everyone* does.

I reach for my dress again, but he holds up his hand to stop me. Then he looks behind him to everyone at the table. I'd forgotten they were there since the moment his presence took up all the breathing room in front of me.

I hate that my heart rate picks up being near him, but not because I'm frightened.

How fucked-up am I to be thinking of how large his cock might be while I know for a fact he kills the women he fucks.

That should be a big turn off.

Yet, my body betrays me and wants to know what it would be like.

27

Evil bitch.

I don't even know why my body is feeling this way to begin with, considering a man has never made me come.

"Leave."

They do as he says. Chairs scrape instantly, all of them standing in unison and then walking out the back door.

He waits and watches before he turns back to me. "You ruined my night, so you better be making it up to me."

Again, I say nothing. He moves away and rests on the table's edge behind him, his legs stretching out and crossing as his gaze now fully roams every part of me.

His eyes show me shades of a forest, the dark earth of the trees. Like deep within the woods, where it's scary, Lucas is the same. He takes you out there, fucks you, then burns your body when he's done. Your ashes scattered among the dirt floor, leaving you a worthless memory.

I begin to approach him as I reach for the hem of my dress once again, to which he raises a brow.

"Can't say I've had trash for a long time."

He did *not* say that.

Did he?

He just called me trash.

Fuck him, the asshole.

"Can't say I've had fucked-up, asshole maniac

either, but look where we are." His legs uncross and spread before him at my words. "And that's saying something for a whore," I spit at him. Lucas sucks in a breath, taking two swift steps up to me. His hand lands on my hip and he grips it hard before it slides it down over my ass.

"Where are your panties, whore?"

I inch closer to his face, so we are almost nose-to-nose. "In my last customer's pocket." I smirk. It's a lie, but he doesn't have to know that.

"You've already finished work for the day, then. That means I can abuse this cunt?" His hand goes to slide around to my bare pussy, but I stop him.

"That's a no." With my other hand, I pull my dress up. He looks down between us, and as he does, I lean in and bite his cheek.

"Love bites. Can't say I've had those for a while," he growls in my ear, and that's exactly where I need his attention to be.

I take a deep breath and do the stupidest thing I could possibly ever do, and *that's* really saying something. I pull the knife out of the strap on my leg and bring it to his throat, adjusting my body out of his grasp.

"You can't afford me," I tell him. "And I know better than to give it away for free." I look him up and down, as he's done to me. "Especially to you."

A slow and steady smirk touches his lips, and he moves closer to me, the knife pressing into his skin. I watch in horror as he pushes more and more until blood starts seeping slowly from his neck, forming little droplets.

"If you plan to pull a knife on me, you'd better back it up."

I press harder, feeling it cut deeper.

Do I really plan to kill a member of the mafia? Especially when they all know what I look like.

"You are scum."

"Coming from a prostitute," he bites back.

Yes, I may sell myself for money, but there's a reason why I am this way. One he would never understand.

"Fuck you."

"Oh, I plan to *fuck you*. Maybe not today, but mark my words, I'll be between those legs in no time." He licks his lips and takes a step back from me, the knife removing from his flesh. I see the blood dripping down his throat into the opening of his shirt, and he makes no move to clean it away. He simply reaches behind him and picks up a cigar, putting it to his lips as he watches me. "If I were you, I'd run before I change my mind." He clicks his tongue.

I back away until my ass hits the door, then I reach for the handle and turn without a second's hesitation. As soon as it opens, I'm out. The bartender smiles at me as I run, my feet aching and my heels clicking, but I don't stop until I'm safely in my car. The stupid thing starts, which I thank the stars for.

As soon as I get to the shitty apartment complex I call home, I take the stairs to the second floor and swing the door open to find my brother sitting in front of the television with a bag of popcorn open, watching a movie.

"What the fuck were you thinking?" I scream at him.

He jumps in surprise, popcorn flying everywhere, as his head whips toward me.

I slam the door and storm over to him, shoving my hand in his face. "You little shit. I fucking warned you."

Brody rolls his eyes and focuses back on his movie.

"I had to," he mutters.

"Had to?" I bite back.

"Yes. You aren't happy. I know you do what you do because of me. And he pays well," Brody states, simply, still not looking my way.

"It doesn't matter if I'm happy. I didn't sign a deal with the monster," I reply.

"You didn't? Seems to me you did. You've been saying all month it's your last night. Yet, here you are." He waves his hand up and down, making a point about my outfit.

"The money's too good to pass up." The words leave me on a stolen breath. It's an excuse but also

31

the truth. Working at a small clothing boutique during the day just isn't cutting it. Feeding two people and paying for a roof over our heads requires extra cash.

"Well, so is mine." Brody pulls out a wad of cash from his pocket and throws it on the floor. "Now, quit like you said you were going to because I can help now."

"No, you're going to college. That's the plan," I bite back at him.

"I'm not. I dropped out of school a month ago." My jaw hits the floor—this was not *our* plan.

Not *our plan* at all.

How could he do that to me? To us. After everything we've worked for.

"Chanel." He says my name and stands. Brody's taller than me now, and not so much my baby brother anymore. Though he will always be to me. "I can help. Let me help now."

"I don't want this life for you. It was meant to be different for you," I say on a broken whisper.

"There's no escaping this life, only surviving it," he replies. I want to argue with him and tell him how wrong he is, but the words get stuck in the back of my throat. How can I tell him he's wrong when our mother and father couldn't escape this life no matter how much they tried? It seems our chances are slim to none.

No matter how hard I try to change Brody's

path, it seems that it's impossible, and I hate that fact. I hate that for him, and I hate that for us.

We didn't plan it to be this way. But somehow, we haven't been able to crawl out of the hole our parents left us permanently buried in.

I try to remember good memories of both of them, but every time I do, all I remember are bad ones.

The only good memories I have are of Brody and me.

It's just us.

Always has been.

"I've been doing that. Surviving," I say quietly. "For the both of us."

"And now you can stop doing that and only work at the boutique. I can earn cash, and we can both pitch in, instead of just you."

"I can make ends meet on my own. Go back to school."

He shrugs. "Can't. Got kicked out."

My mouth drops open again. Seems I am doing that a lot as I learn more and more about what Brody's been up to. "What for?"

"I may have run a guy's head through the bathroom wall."

I…I don't even know what to say to that. How on earth…

"Why?" I manage to ask. He rubs his hand down his face and looks away, mumbling something unintelligible. "Brody," I push through gritted teeth.

"Because he called *you* a *whore*." I step back and sit on our ratty old chair. I can't say I blame him. I've beaten people up for less than speaking ill of my brother.

"Well, that sucks."

He turns away and looks back to the television. "Yep," is all he says in return.

I sit there watching Brody for a while before my mind drifts to *him*.

Lucas.

I know he'll make me pay for what I did. No one threatens him, let alone makes him bleed.

Stories are told all over the place regarding Lucas, and trust me when I say none of them are ever good. He may not be the leader of the mafia, but that does not make him weak. He runs our part of town with an iron fist, everyone knows his name, and everyone knows not to be anywhere near him.

Women who have supposedly been with him have turned up dead. They say that his bedroom antics are rough and not for the faint-hearted. He likes blood, he likes to tie his women up. I'm sure there are many other things too, but that's the main gist of what goes around about Lucas Rossi.

A fist bangs on my door, and both Brody's and my eyes snap to our entrance.

"Bitch, open up." I watch as relief surges

through Brody, then he gets up and walks to his room, shutting the door. Standing and kicking off my heels, I pull the door open to find my friend, who is also a hooker, waiting there. She flicks her braids behind her ears and steps in, looking around. When her dark eyes land on me, she purses her lips.

"You had to go and be a complete idiot."

News spreads fast around here.

"What?" I ask her, feigning innocence. Merci and I have been friends for as long as I can remember. She lives in the same apartment building as us. If you can even call them apartments, more like shit boxes. When I had to go to work, she would come over and sit with Brody. Merci has her grandmother, and that's it. She didn't start hooking until way after I started, and that's only because her granny took ill.

"Do not 'what' me, woman. What the fuck? Everyone is talking." I sit back down and lay my head in my hands. "He doesn't play, girl, you know this. He's a serpent. Evil as they come."

"He doesn't know who I am."

She throws her head back and laughs. Her dark skin has body glitter spread all over it, making her shine beautifully.

"Oh, he does. It's why his car is parked out front right now."

Oh, fuck no. I run to the window and look outside, and there he is, leaning against his car, a cigarette between his lips, as he looks up at the building.

"I would get away from the window. I don't think he knows which one is yours… yet."

Thinking she's right, because he would be in here already, I duck down, then lift up on my knees and peek out. I see him talking to a neighbor's kid, then watch in horror as the kid points to my window. His eyes lock on mine, and I fall backward at the steely glare he sends my way.

"He moves fast," I breathe out.

"You didn't really think he wouldn't, did you?"

"Shut up. And get out before he comes up." I push her, but she brushes me off.

"Hand me one of your guns. I'll sit with Brody."

That's friendship right there.

But…

"I can't drag you into this." She waves a hand over her shoulder.

"I'm already in this. Now, give me a gun, and I'll let you handle him." I reach for one and place it in her waiting palm. She checks that it's loaded before she goes into Brody's room, and just as she does, a knock is heard on the door.

It's not hard and fast like Merci's, but it's there.

"Chanel Lilly. What a beautiful name." I freeze at his voice.

"Lucas Rossi. What a feral name."

He goes silent on the other side of the door. "Should I kick the door in, or do you plan to open it?" he asks after a moment of silence. "I'll give you to five, but be warned, you will have made me extra fucking furious."

Then he starts counting.

One.

Two.

My feet carry me toward the door.

Three.

I touch the handle.

Four.

Bracing myself, I pull it open to see Lucas standing there. He looks me over and then walks in, pushing straight past me, kicking the door shut behind him.

I'm frozen in place as he strides around, his eyes assessing my space before they come back to land on me. "Nice shithole."

I can't deny his words, it is a shithole. But I attempt to keep it clean, at least.

"Now, would you like to talk here, or in the bedroom?"

CHAPTER FOUR

CHANEL

*W*hat the fuck?

"Here," I bite back.

He looks over my shoulder to Brody's bedroom, then quickly closes the few feet between us and Brody's door. Once his hand is covering the knob, he turns and looks back at me, a serious but somehow slightly playful look in his eyes.

"I don't like company," he says, then opens the door.

I step up behind him to see Brody on his bed, with Merci next to him, pointing the gun at the door.

"I would put that down and leave," he commands.

Neither of them move a muscle.

I slip in next to him, my side touching his as I

look at them. "You should go. Go to Merci's and I'll stay here."

Brody's eyes lock on mine, and I see the worry etched there.

Merci goes to speak, but I hold up my hand. "I'll be there after, I promise." She still doesn't seem convinced. Lucas stays quiet next to me, so I walk in and grab the gun from her hand as she gets up.

She leans in. "Shoot first, ask questions later," she whispers. I know what she's talking about. There have been a lot of rapes in the area, and all of us women have been carrying weapons of some sort around with us. But I have a feeling Lucas doesn't need to rape a woman.

"I'd advise against that. I'm hard to kill," Lucas replies, overhearing what she said.

Merci pulls back and reaches for Brody's hand, tugging him out the door.

I turn to face Lucas. "I'm sure a bullet to your brain would suffice."

"You'd have to aim it at me first." He licks his lips.

I hear the front door shut and I do just that. Lifting the gun, the safety already off, I aim. But before I can get it at his height, he has disarmed me.

How in the hell?

"I'd punish for a lot less," he rasps, then takes the gun to the counter, removes the bullets, and places it down as if it's an everyday occurrence for him.

"Why are you here?" I ask as he steps back over to me. The cut on his throat is still red, blood now dried in a neat line, but he doesn't seem to care. He leans in and smells me, before pulling back and sitting on the sofa. His hands splay out against the back of it, and he locks those eyes on me.

I don't move from where I'm standing, waiting for him to say, or do, whatever he came here to. But then his gaze drifts to my bathroom and he nods to it. The door is open, and from where he's sitting, he can see the shower-bath cubicle inside.

"Get naked and bath yourself. You're dirty." His eyes roam me. "I can smell other men on you."

"I'd rather have a bath with a toaster turned on than one with you."

"Strip."

"I'm not fucking you or having a bath with you."

"Strip," he repeats.

I huff out a breath and place my hand on my dress strap, letting it drop, then do the same with the other. While I shimmy it down my body, my hair tickles my back, until I'm standing in front of him in nothing but the strap on my leg that holds the knife I cut him with. I'm sure his blood is still on the blade. I go to remove it, but he speaks.

"Leave it." I let my arms hang at my sides as I

stand there, naked and unashamed. I'm not shy about my body. I was a dancer all through school, so I have toned legs and a great ass. My tits aren't very large, but they're flattering on my smaller frame.

"I'm not fucking you," I say again.

He waves his hand in a circle.

"Turn."

I do, slowly, trying to keep him in my sights the whole time. For all I know, the minute my eyes are off him, he'll put a bullet in the back of my head.

But once my back is to him, he speaks again, "Stop."

I do and look over my shoulder. His eyes have darkened, and his hands are clenched.

"Bend over and touch your toes." His voice stays the same, with no change in his tone. Like this is the kind of request he makes everyday.

"We aren't doing *Ring Around the Rosie*," I say snarkily. He shuts me up from saying any more with a sharp glare.

"Bend," he commands, angrier now.

"So fucking bossy," I mutter to myself and do as he asks. Granted, I've been asked for worse. I once had a guy pay me five thousand to shit on his chest. Do you know how hard it is to force a shit with someone watching you?

It's fucked.

Bending over is a walk in the park.

Until *him*.

Because for some reason, he makes me feel even more naked than I am, and that's not possible. Considering I am butt-ass naked.

"Stand." I do as he says. He indicates with a finger for me to come to him. When I reach him, he looks up at me again. "Turn." Again, I follow his instruction. *Fucking hell, what game is he playing?* "Stop." My ass is more than likely in his face. "Now, bend." If I do, my ass will literally be in his face, no doubt about that at all.

"Are you serious?" I ask, not quite shocked but completely bewildered.

"Did you come into my establishment and cut me?" he barks.

"Yes."

"Now, bend." I relent and do as he says, then a second of silence later, I feel him right there. At my entrance. But he doesn't touch me, just breathes me in.

What the fuck is wrong with him?

And why does it turn me on?

He takes his time, and when I feel him pull away, I stand and turn around to face him.

"You can leave now." I'm impressed that my voice doesn't come out shaky at my demand.

Lucas stands before I can even think to move, and he grabs me by my throat, looking me in the eyes. My breathing picks up and I feel my heart start racing in my chest—I like his hands on me. I hate his hands on me. His other hand comes down on my thigh, stopping me from grabbing my knife, and he whispers against my mouth, "It's a dangerous thing to play with the viper." He runs his tongue along his lips and it's not a kiss, more of a taste, my breath hitching at the sensation. "Once we have a taste, we become addicted to the poison. And then, there is no escape." I close my eyes at his touch, and when his lips leave mine, he pulls back and stares at me. "You like it. You're just as fucked-up as I am."

Then he turns and walks out the door, leaving me standing there, naked and wondering what the fuck just happened. And why I didn't hate it.

⸙

*A*s they walk in the door, I manage to pull my dress down. Brody shakes his head as he looks me over and Merci just locks eyes with me.

"What did he make you do?" she asks, her arms crossing over her chest.

Fuck that! I don't want to tell her. How would I even begin to do that? I mean, I've told her everything I do for clients, including the down-right dirty shit, but somehow this feels…different.

"Don't worry."

Her eyes pinch and she looks to Brody.

"I didn't mean for this to happen," Brody says, lifting his hand and rubbing the back of his head. I forget that he's almost a grown man. When I look back to Merci, I see her biting her lip.

"It's fine. Go watch a movie. I'm gonna shower and change."

Brody nods and goes to his room.

"He's trying, you know. He knows what you have to deal with."

"He got kicked out of school." I huff and walk into the kitchen, more than a little fed up with everything right now. I unclip the strap around my thigh and put the knife on the counter. She looks at it, and her brows pinch.

"What did you do?" She picks it up. "It has blood on it."

"His blood," I tell her.

She drops the knife like it's on fire and shakes her head.

"You know better than that, Chanel. Why would you do that? Are you wanting us to bury you?" She grinds her teeth and then takes in a long breath.

"No. Brody shouldn't have been there. He knows better." I try to keep my voice low, so Brody doesn't hear me.

Merci shakes her head, glances back to the knife, then whispers, "What did you do?"

I shrug, as if it's nothing. "I put the knife to his throat."

She gasps so loudly that Brody opens his door and looks out. When he sees it's just us, he goes back into his room and shuts the door again.

"This can't happen. You need to pack your shit and we need to work out where you can go, because now you're on his hit list, and we know everyone who turns up on his list ends up dead."

"I have nowhere to go," I respond on an exasperated sigh.

And I'm not lying when I say those words. I literally have nowhere to go. Our parents were both only children, and they hardly had any friends. It was Brody and me, no one else. It's pretty much the same thing now, the only difference being that I have Merci, who's practically a sister to me. She's helped me so much with Brody. I don't know what I would've done without her.

I shrug, and she does this thing where she sucks her bottom lip in, then pops it out, before she turns and walks back to our tattered little couch, sitting down and groaning.

"He *will* kill you." I should be worried because what she says is what we know is the truth. Lucas is, as he says, a viper, with large extendable fangs that can reach anywhere.

A viper hunts, they strike, then they kill.

And I absolutely hate the fact that he's the first

man ever in my life to make me feel something other than *it's just sex*. Yes, it would still be just that, but why did my stomach flutter when he was near?

And why is he so good-looking?

It has to be because of the power he holds, right? Or maybe it's just my concern and my body is acting a different way to protect myself. Yeah, that has to be it.

I understand the appeal toward him now, though. Why he's whispered about. I always thought it was a joke. I mean, some women even want to risk their own lives to be with him. What a bunch of idiots.

"As long as he doesn't kill Brody, that's all I care about."

Merci shakes her head at that. I've never really lived this life for me. I dropped out of school to look after Brody. I sold myself—my body—so I could put a roof over our heads and food in our mouths. When you love someone and you come from nothing, you will do anything possible just to have *something*. No matter how shoddy this place is, it's what we call home. And to Brody, it's his safe place. No work comes here, no drama comes here—it's just Merci and us.

Until Lucas.

"You know Brody's right. He is old enough now to help. To pitch in. You were what? Seventeen, when you started?" I nod my head. It's been years, and I stopped for a while, then started back up again. The money was good, and in the end, it was the only way. It's like a hit of some drug. You tell yourself it's only once, but you keep going back for more, and more.

"I don't want the same for Brody," I tell her. "You know this."

"Brody isn't going to sell his body." Merci waves a hand, dismissing me.

"No, just his soul to the damn devil," I complain, already knowing the truth. I bite the inside of my cheek as I look at her.

"That may be true, but I think that devil wants your soul more than his, hunny."

I have a feeling her words are true—that it's me he wants, and I don't know how I feel about that. Will I be another girl on the news they find dead? Or maybe he'll keep me and play with me longer. Which fate is worse, I don't know.

I'm not even sure I want to find out.

But I doubt I'll have much of a choice after tonight.

I don't think Lucas gives anyone choices.

CHAPTER FIVE

LUCAS

*T*hat little honey. All the ways I plan to fuck her have been on my mind since the moment she shut the door in the back room of the bar. I had to watch and assess just to see what type of woman she was, and to say she didn't disappoint would be an understatement. Just thinking about her makes my cock hard. And the way she smells… fuck! I could've come on the fucking spot. That's sweet fucking pussy.

I'm a taker. That's what I am in this life. I see something, I fucking take it. And if anyone stops me, I'll end their fucking life.

I wasn't raised with a silver spoon in my mouth —mine was motherfucking gold.

Yes, you read that right. Because not only am I a mommy's boy with daddy issues—which I will happily tell you about—I'm a fucking spoiled brat and always get what I want.

But let's make no mistake.

I play dirty.

Just because I had a helping hand, does not mean I didn't work for everything I have.

I'm not trusted to run the area I do just out of luck. I built it up, made them fear me, then I came to own them. And I did a lot of bad shit to get here.

Some would be ashamed, feel guilt.

Not me.

I could give two flying fucks what you think. You see me giving you the finger. Good, sit on it and motherfucking spin for all I care.

Because not only could I buy you too, but I would slice your throat and have you begging for my cock at the same time.

Want to know why? Because I've done it.

But not once have I had the same thing happen to me.

Until *her.*

I haven't seen her for weeks, but I've been watching. Stalking her.

The door opens to my bar, and I see the young guy walk in. The little brother, who I'm pretty sure she told to stay far, far away from here.

His hands are in his pockets, and he looks around as he closes the door behind him. When he glances up, he sees me sitting at the bar with a glass in my hand and walks over to me, his head down.

"Do you have any work?"

Goddammit! This kid has balls.

Does he know what his sister did to get him out of here? I guess not, otherwise he wouldn't be standing right there.

Unless he plans to kill me.

Which I highly doubt.

I eye him up and down. He's not scrawny, he's got some muscle on him, and he is dressed in clothes that are probably bought from a thrift shop. His shoes have holes in them, but somehow, he radiates confidence. *I wonder if he gets it from her?*

"Do you have a death wish?" I retort.

Mario walks out from the door to the bar and stops when he sees the kid and me. I wave him off and he goes back from where he came, leaving us alone.

"I need the money."

"And what do you need said money for?" I ask him in return.

He scratches the back of his hand, like he needs to think about that answer. A smart boy. "What is it you need done?"

"That isn't what I asked you," I bite back.

He nods and lowers his head. "Anything but fuck a guy."

"Have you ever done that? You never know, you

may enjoy it." His eyes go wide, and he shakes his head infinitesimally. "Relax, I won't ask you to fuck anyone, kid."

"I'm an adult," he replies. "Just turned eighteen today."

"Is this why you're back, instead of listening to your sister?"

He nods.

I don't understand their relationship as I'm an only child. It's probably best that's the case anyway. The closest people I have to brothers are Keir and Joey, but even those two have their own stupid fucking bromance. Keir may want to kill him most of the time, just like I'm sure he wants to kill me too.

"She doesn't have to know."

"Oh, I think she'll find out." I stare at him, and he says nothing. "I can't have your sister in here threatening my people. She may end up fucking dead otherwise."

He swallows and then nods his head. "I got it."

"You can start tomorrow. We have a game on. Same as last time."

"Thank you, Lucas."

I grind my teeth. "It's sir, not Lucas," I snap at him.

"Sorry. Sir, yes… of course."

I hate it when people use my name, it's one of my biggest fucking peeves. Only my family can get away with it, and even then, it grinds on everything in me.

He turns and starts to make his way to the door. "Kid."

He stops mid-step and looks back.

"Tell your sister I expect to see her later tonight to speak with me, because we both know she will."

He nods again and hurries to leave.

Now it's just a matter of time before her sweet ass walks through that door.

And I'll wait.

For something that sweet, I'll play any game.

As long as I win, of course.

And we all know I *will* win.

CHAPTER SIX

CHANEL

*F*ucking hell.

I swear, it's just that I don't usually swear this much. But with him, I just can't help myself.

It's the similar scene, different day. Lucas is waiting out front for me, his back leaning against his car with that stupid cigarette in his mouth. I walk straight up to him and pull it from his lips, throwing it to the ground. Guns are pulled on me from either side and aimed at my head, but I take no notice. Because I have a feeling he doesn't want me dead, not just yet anyway.

"You really had to hire him?"

Lucas' eyes skim me, then he licks his lips. "Yes, you are late." That's the extent of his reply.

I've gone a week without seeing him.

I would rather go a week more.

No scrub that, forever would be better!

But Brody is eighteen now, and legally, he can work. So why am I trying to stop him? It's not like the money won't help us.

"Fire him," I demand, my hands crossing over my chest.

Lucas waves and the guys who had the guns trained at my head lower them and walk away, leaving us by ourselves outside the front of his club. It's dark and no one is on the streets because everyone knows what danger lurks here.

Him.

It's *him* they are all afraid of.

"What will I get in return?" he asks, the question pulling a smirk from his lips.

"I won't fuck you. I know what you do to women you fuck."

"Do you, now?" He quirks a brow. "What do I do?"

"Most wind up dead."

"Only the bad ones." The sick bastard winks. "Are you bad?"

"Yes. So what do you want?"

"Nothing. I'm not firing him." He moves around me to go back into the club, but not before taking his time to give my appearance a thorough once-over. I'm dressed pretty much the same as I was the last time I saw him. I didn't plan to work today, but someone offered me over five hundred bucks cash that I couldn't refuse for a hand job. He was desperate. And it seems, so am I. But I plan on purchasing Brody a pair of Nike Air Force 1 shoes he's been eyeing for months that we could never afford.

"Fire him."

He spins and is in front of me in the blink of an eye. He's taller, so his eyes look down as they lock on mine. It really is like entering the woods when you lock eyes with him; you know you should look away and run toward the light, but you're stuck in there, lost in the dark.

"No one tells me what to do, not even my mother," he spits out at my face in anger.

"Keir," I state, knowing full well who his boss is.

"He knows better. Only when I'm with him do I listen." I say nothing in return. "Even then, I choose not to. Remember that."

"My brother's just a kid," I plead giving him my best doe-eyes.

"As I'm sure you were the first time you spread your legs."

Damn! He's got me there.

"I'll do it."

"Do what, please say?" Lucas asks, then he backs away from me, putting distance between us.

"Whatever it is you want." The words leave my mouth in such a rush I feel lightheaded.

"Don't act like it would be a chore to fuck me. I

saw your reaction the other night. You want it, but you're afraid." He steps back up to me takes a strand of my hair and pushes it behind my ear before he leans in and whispers in my ear, "And you should be."

Then he pulls away, and heads right back toward the entrance, yelling over his shoulder. "Offer denied! Tell your brother I'll see him tonight. And not to be late. I once cut a man's finger off for tardiness." With that, he strides through the door to his club, leaving me standing on the street to wonder what's next.

The asshole.

Trailing after him, I slide through the closing door and watch him disappear through the hallway to the back.

It's then the bartender walks out, holding a carton of beer with a name tag that reads Marcus. He stops when he sees me and shakes his head. "You totally have a death wish, girl." His eyes assess me, though.

"Or, you know, he's just an asshole."

"Oh, that he is. But most women don't come back several times unless they're fucking him. Which, clearly, you are not, considering you have no marks on you." I look down over my body. I'm wearing a small red dress that shows plenty of skin. I got it from a thrift shop where Merci and I go once every few months, so we aren't wearing the same things continuously. I don't wear dresses unless I'm working. But when I do, it's usually all the same style—short and sassy.

"He kills them," I state.

"Amongst other things," he says, laughing. "Like I said, *death wish*." Then he walks off to where I have no care and I realize I'm not in the mood to deal with him any longer today.

᠅

*W*hen I get home after making a quick stop, Brody is about to leave. He throws on his jacket then slides his wallet into his pocket. He told me earlier he'd be heading to the bar to work, and to say I was furious would be an understatement.

"You can quit your second job now. Do the other full-time."

"Not going to happen, because you can't work for him," I declare.

"Oh, by the way, I forgot to tell you earlier, Lucas said you need to come in and see him," Brody tells me.

I reply with, "I've already seen Lucas once to many times today, so no, I won't be coming in."

Brody says, "When you see him, you need to call him sir, not Lucas."

Ha! Not fucking likely. I'll stick to *that asshole*.

"I got you something," I say, handing him a bag.

Brody looks at it and pulls his brows together. "Um… we don't do presents."

"I know, but this time it's special. The big one eight," I say, smiling.

With that he nods and opens the bag. When he sees the box, he pulls it out like a kid at Christmas time. "Shit, sis."

"Brody," I warn him.

He smiles so big at the shoes that all I can do is smile right along with him when he pulls me in for a hug. I hug him back before he pulls away, takes a seat and changes his shoes. When he finally has them on, he stands in front of me. "Badass." He nods his head.

"Totally badass," I agree with him.

"Don't be mad, okay? But I heard he's actually good to work for. He pays well if his employees listen. And I'm a great listener."

Instantly, I want to argue with him that he isn't, but I keep my mouth shut. Because he does have to do things on his own. It's time for me to stop mollycoddling him. He's an adult now, as he so likes to remind me.

"Good luck," I manage to say. "If you get yourself killed or hurt, I'm afraid I'll be going down with you."

Brody nods and pulls on his jacket, and when

the door shuts beind him, I'm left to worry if I will see my baby brother after tonight.

❧

*M*erci lets herself in about an hour into my attempt to distract myself with a movie. "So, where's Brody?"

I'm sitting on the couch with my legs tucked under me when I answer her. "He's at work," I reply, not taking my attention away from the television, and she plops down next to me.

"You let him go? Wow! Didn't think you would, and he would have to sneak out."

"I thought about it, not letting him go," I tell her honestly. "I went to see Lucas." She reaches for the remote and switches off the television. My cell starts ringing, but I ignore it as I wait for her to say something.

"He's dangerous. And…he is clearly interested in you."

I go to argue, but I can't because he is.

"What happened when he was here?" I look away and back to the dark television screen.

"He made me bend over in front of him."

"Okay, that's not too bad."

"Then he smelled me." Her eyes go wide and her head juts back, in a kind of disgust versus curiosity look. "Between my legs...while I was naked," I say on a whisper.

"That boy has some kink, and I think that kink may be you." She chuckles.

My cell starts ringing again, and this time, I get up to answer it. I have one of those cheap flip phones, not the iPhones everyone else uses. I can't afford one and see them as a waste of money.

"Hello." Music blares over the line and then my brother's voice comes through.

"Come down, they're throwing me a party."

*Okay...*I look to the phone in confusion, then to Merci.

"He says they're throwing him a party and I should join them," I tell her, my brows furrowing.

It doesn't take long before she's standing with a smile on her face. "Right, let's go."

"You literally just said he's dangerous."

She claps her hands together. "But sometimes we all need to take a walk on the wild side, don't we?" She heads to the door and calls over her shoulder, "I'm going to get changed, and you and me...we're going to drink while the night is young."

"I'm not changing," I yell out to her but she's gone.

I sit back on the couch and wait until she walks back in. She does a twirl and shows off the gorgeous yellow dress that sits at her knees and has a slit up the side. Yellow looks amazing on her. I get up and pocket my cell as I walk to the door.

"You really need to step up your style." She flicks her braids behind her head, and I hold back the laughter itching to burst from my mouth. It was a struggle to get me into those dresses she made me wear to begin with. But the bonus about dresses is that they're faster to get on after the sex, so I wear them. But when I'm home, it's jeans, track pants, or just a shirt long enough to cover my ass.

"I look fine," I reply and smile as we get into her beat-up car. She turns the key, and it doesn't start. I sit there as she hits the dash, then does it again. This time, it starts and we both sigh in relief.

It's late, and I figured Brody would be home by now, but he's eighteen and it is his birthday so I have to cut him some slack. And Merci says he needs a little fun in his life.

"I got him those shoes," I tell her.

"So you took a job today?" she asks.

"Yep."

"Thought you were quitting."

I shrug and look out the window into the night.

"Do it. You hate it. And I know you have some money saved, so use that if you have to."

"Why don't you stop?" I ask, in a genuine effort to get the heat off me.

"Because, unlike you, I like the job." She

puckers her lips. "The money, the sex, every single part of it."

"Has one ever made you come?" I ask, thinking of how it felt to have Lucas near me.

"Only this one man who, might I add, pays the best. Always asks for me, usually once a month, and I never, ever, turn him down. Then, after him I will turn everything down for a week, so as to not ruin the memory."

Finally, she comes to a stop out front of Lucas' club. It looks dead, but with the window down I can hear the music blaring out here from inside.

"Are we really doing this?" I bite my cheek as the nerves hit me at the thought of seeing Lucas after our interaction.

"We are. It's Brody's birthday and he wants you there." She gets out first and I follow. I pull at my hair bun to tighten it as we walk to the entrance, but as we go to step in, the doors are pushed open and the same guy from earlier is standing there.

"About time." He holds it open for us and we step through.

We're instantly hit with the smell of smoke and alcohol.

"Take this." He hands me a bottle of beer, which I pass to Merci, and I keep on going until I see Brody. He's at the back where a karaoke machine is located. I don't recognize anyone else. I can tell he's had a few to drink. Which, I might add, is illegal. Though, everything in this bar probably is, so no surprises there.

"Killing it, Brody," Merci screams, throwing her fist up in the air. There are probably twenty people here, and all twenty seem to look back at the sound of her voice all at once. I cringe and step back, shaking my head, but Merci doesn't care as she continues to move closer to him.

"Different attire."

My back straightens at *his* voice, goosebumps tickle all over my skin, and I freeze.

CHAPTER SEVEN

LUCAS

*S*he's hard to miss. Even dressed in jeans and a baggy white shirt, her hair back, and those hypnotizing eyes with those fuckable lips that I know would look good wrapped around my cock.

Her friend makes her way to her brother, and I step up behind her. I stand there for a few seconds just watching her, tasting the air that she consumes in the hopes I can taste her in it.

When I speak, I watch as her whole body locks up. She ignores me, keeping her back to me. So I step closer, my head lowering to her neck and taking in a deep breath.

"You are so fucking weird. Who goes around sniffing people?" she questions, turning her head and pinning me with those chocolate eyes, makes me want to bend her over and taste every inch of her starting with that smart-ass mouth. When I don't answer her, she turns back around and looks at her brother. "Why did you do this for him?"

"I gave him new shoes too, but it seems you beat me to it." This time when she turns to me, a different look passes over her face. "It wasn't for sympathy or because I care. He looked like trash, and my employees are not allowed to look like trash."

She blinks a few times, like she's trying to understand all my words and put them into context, but then she says exactly what she wants to. "You're a real ass."

"So I've been told."

"I really don't want him working for you. The last thing I need is to be identifying his body."

"You've done this before?"

"My parents," she confirms and looks away again. I hate when those eyes aren't on me, assessing me, trying to figure out the 'real' me.

And what is this fascination I have for her?

Why do I want to bend her over right now and fuck her, but only after I taste her first?

"I would give my condolences, but I don't really care," I tell her.

Her next words surprise me. "Neither do I. And the last thing I would want from you is sympathy.

Keep it and shove it." She goes to step away from me, but I capture her hand. Her head whips back to see where we're joined, then her gaze moves to my face, and I squeeze her fingers, pinning her with a stare.

"I'll have you, you know that, right? And not by buying you either."

Chanel pulls her hand away from mine. "If that's what you think. The only way you're getting this is by payment. And lucky for me, you can't afford me no matter the price." She turns and saunters off to where her friend and brother are currently seated.

"Sir." I don't bother turning to face Sergio. Sergio has been with me since I was a teenager, but he isn't family. And trust me when I say, everyone hated that fact. It's a family business, what we do. And even then, if they aren't, it's in a contract of a friend or a family member. We always make sure we have something over someone. And I do over Sergio, but I've never had to use it and don't think I'll ever have to. He's too loyal.

"Boss is on his way. You want to clear things out?"

I look back to where she's standing near the stage with her brother. When Keir comes, he likes to talk in private, not that he comes here all that often. But tonight I don't want to kick her out, so I turn to Sergio. "No. Watch that one." I nod to Chanel, then walk out the back where I know Keir's car will arrive. Everyone who's currently in the back scatters and leaves. I hold the door open as I watch his car come to a stop. It starts raining, but it doesn't bother him. Joey gets out and walks over first, followed by Keir. Joey is Keir's younger brother, and Keir's our boss. He's one of the only men I respect, and that's saying a lot since I hate almost everyone.

"You're open," Joey says, obviously hearing the music. I nod and show them in. "What's the occasion?" he asks, raising one brow.

I ignore him and look at Keir. "What brings you here?" I ask.

Joey heads out to the bar and then it's just the two of us. I sit down at the round table, and he pulls out a seat and sits across from me.

"It seems Romarc's men are angry." He leans forward, hands on the table, fingers tapping on the surface. "Apparently, me killing him didn't appease everyone."

I huff.

Romarc was a supplier. He sold and distributed, then he thought, stupidly, that he could outwit Keir.

No one outwits Keir.

That ended with him dead.

But I like to think the real reason he ended up

dead was that he took an interest in Keir's wife, Sailor, who Keir just so happens to be obsessed with. He wasn't meant to marry her. He had a contract signed by his father and another family that stated he was meant to marry Paige. But it turns out Paige is one hell of a crazy bitch, and by that stage, he was already in love with Sailor.

We all knew it wasn't going to stand—the contract, that is.

It just took Keir a while longer to figure out how to get around it. Because he follows his rules, and he absolutely loves what he does. He is the most feared and untouchable man, and you would be stupid to cross him. His temper is short. Not as bad as mine, but he is more calculated.

"And you want me to do what?" I ask him.

His fingers tap again, and he looks me dead in the eyes. "Clean it up." He stands, then walks to the door that leads to the bar, and I follow him. Joey's at the bar and next to him is Chanel. I push past Keir and stalk over to her. She notices me first and sighs heavily as I approach.

"Nice talking to you." She smiles at Joey, and I bristle at that. She then proceeds to give me the stink eye as her gaze falls to me, before she takes off.

"Why are you watching her like that?" Joey asks, eyes locked on me.

"Like what?" I ask, turning to face him.

"Like you plan to fuck her."

I've thought about it, multiple times. Even right now, I want her. To bend her over to taste and smell that sweet-ass pussy. Her taste is going to be immaculate. And knowing me—because I clearly have an addictive personality—I'll become hooked.

On her.

Which would be new.

When I fuck a woman, I'll maybe go back for seconds, but rarely thirds. Then I either dispose of them or leave them, depending on who they are, of course.

It's not that I have a thing about fucking the same woman once or twice. No, it's more about…

… her smell changes.

And I can't fucking stand it.

I once killed a man who was a doctor. He told me I had hyperosmia. It has to do with smell. A hyperosmiac is someone who has an overwhelming or heightened sense of smell. At the time he told me I should seek help, but to me, smell is everything.

I'm sure most cases of hyperosmia aren't like mine.

I can only fuck someone if she smells right.

It doesn't matter to me about weight, color, or appearance, it's all about how they smell, and how they continue to smell.

And I am not fucking around when I tell you, Chanel smells like the best thing on this fucking earth.

So I have to take my time.

See if her smell changes.

See how I feel about that.

Because the last thing she needs is me addicted to her.

As things I get addicted to end up dead.

"I t's time to go," I say to Brody. He's been drinking, which he shouldn't have been. But I highly doubt the police are going to burst into this bar.

Only the stupid think about coming here.

Like me.

"But Lucas said I can drink as much as I want. And they say he's never this nice." I look over my shoulder to where *he* stands at the bar with Joey, and both of their gazes are locked on me.

The door that Lucas came out of opens and a man dressed in a suit strides out. When I look back to the two men at the bar, they're talking, and the man in the suit eyes me, his brows scrunching as he studies me.

"We need to leave. *Now.* I know who that is,"

Merci says, leaning in next to me. "We shouldn't be here."

"That's what I've been telling you," I reply while shaking my head.

Lucas has his back to me now and is talking to the man in the suit. I eye them separately, both without a doubt good-looking men, and both with dark hair. Lucas is younger, that is obvious, but even for his age, he holds power that almost matches the man standing next to him. Which says a lot, since everyone in this place is now looking everywhere but at him.

"Chanel." The man, Joey, who I spoke to earlier, calls my name. He waves me over, and I hesitate, thinking this is wrong. This could be so very wrong. Merci gives me a small push on my back, and I manage to place one foot in front of the other as I make way over to them. All three sets of eyes lock on me.

"Chanel, this is Keir. He wanted to meet you."

Keir's gaze meets mine before it flicks to Lucas. Lucas' hands slide into his pockets, and Keir watches his reaction before he looks back at me.

"Lucas tells me you're in the service industry." His voice is so deep. "Have you thought about leaving?" It feels like the club has gone silent and it's just us four, the only other sound being my heart beating in my ears.

"Yes," I answer, unsure of why he's asking me this but knowing I should answer.

"My wife is after a sitter and an assistant."

"Boss," Lucas says. When I glance at him I see his jaw is locked tight.

Keir ignores him, focusing solely on me. He nods his head behind me, and I turn to find my brother drunk on the stage.

"That your brother?" he asks, and I nod. "You raised him?" I nod again. "Give Joey your info, he'll be in touch." Keir turns and stalks off, and Joey hands me a business card. I write my full name on it with shaky hands and look up at him. He offers no smile, just gives me a small nod before he follows Keir out of the bar. It would be stupid to say no to a job working for Keir, but also, I'm sure any job is better than my job.

"What have you done?" Lucas seethes. His hand reaches out, and he grips my arm, pulling me toward the back door. He shuts it behind us, pushes my back against it, and cages me in. "Do you know what you've done?"

I want to tell him I have no idea, but instead, I stay quiet and simply stare him. His eyes, which are now dark, seem to penetrate me. His hands are on either side of me, and his lip is turned up in a sneer as he locks eyes with me.

I should be more afraid of him.

Terrified even.

But I'm not.

"I eat women like you for breakfast," he snarls in my face. I go to put my hands on his chest to push him away, but he shakes his head. "I wouldn't touch me if I were you, unless you plan on me fucking you for free." I gasp, then catch myself and roll my eyes. "Because I sure as shit do not pay for sex."

"Like I've said, you couldn't afford me anyway."

He chuckles, and his gaze falls to my lips. "I could, and I will."

"I'll *never* fuck you." My voice is low, but I'm afraid to raise it. Not because I'm afraid of him, but because he might be able to tell what his nearness is doing to me.

It's…dare I say it? Turning me on.

And I hate that.

"Your smell changed." Lucas steps back but keeps his hands on either side of me. I try to shake my head at him, but he moves forward, his face burying into the crook of my neck.

"Get off of me before I knee you where the sun don't shine," I growl. He chuckles again, ignoring me, and drags his nose down my neck until he reaches the swell of my breast, then his hand sneaks out and cups my sex. I gasp at the contact through my jeans.

"The dress gives better access." He peers at me

through his lashes, then pulls his hand away and brings it to his nose and sniffs. A slow but steady smirk plays on his lips. "You're turned on."

How the fuck does he know that?

"No, I'm not," I argue back. He *can't* know that.

"Should we find out?" His hand reaches for the waistband of my jeans and he yanks.

I push his hand away, launch off the door, and poke my finger in his face. "Stop smelling and touching me, you fucking creep." I reach for the door handle, but he's faster than me. He pushes me against the door again and cages me in once more. But this time his front is to my back, and I can feel his cock pressing against my ass.

"But you smell so fucking good." He leans in and doesn't ease up on the pressure I feel behind me. Then he takes another deep breath, and a shiver runs rampant all over my body.

"I'm sure this is classified as assault," I mutter, barely controlling the shakiness of my breath, turning my head and trying to look at him.

"Even if you like it?"

This time he licks my ear.

Is he… tasting me?

"You have the wrong impression. Now I understand where you got that wrong. You think all these women like you, when in reality, we all despise you."

Lucas pushes off me and I feel the cold hit my

back. When I turn around to face him, he's staring at me. His brows furrow as if he is trying to work me out.

"I'm always right when it comes to people," he states.

Is he… defending himself against my words?

"No, I feel they let you believe you're right out of fear."

"You're telling me you don't fear me?" he asks, his head dropping slightly to the side as he quizzes me.

"I feel sorry for you," I reply, standing tall.

This puts a smirk on his lips—not quite a smile, but something more sinister.

"Sugar, you don't feel sorry for me. You want me. But you just don't understand it. Probably because you're so used to spreading those legs for every Tom, Dick, and Harry."

"Sugar?" Distaste fills my mouth. "You don't get the privilege of calling me a nickname." I shake my head. "One…I am *not* fucking you. Two…you can't pay me enough. And three…" I pull open the door, step out, and glance back, "… I fucking hate you."

Walking straight out, I spot Merci and Brody at the bar. I grab both their arms on my way by and pull them toward the door. I look back and Brody starts to protest—until he sees the look on my face.

As soon as the night air hits us, so does the cold.

I take a deep breath and hurry to the car, opening the passenger door for Brody. He pauses, looks over my shoulder, and I know who's there before he says anything. Then, before I can utter a word or even turn around, something hits my head and everything goes black.

*M*y head is sore. That's the first thing I think when my eyes open a tiny crack. I know I didn't drink much, so why does it hurt so badly? I go to lift my hands to touch my head, but I can't. They're stuck. My eyes spring open, and all I see is a white ceiling above me. Moving my head to the side, I'm in a bed, but it's not just any bed, it's the same one I used with my last client. My usual spot.

Why am I here?

"I see you've woken. Took you long enough." There's that voice, Lucas, and I know he's right next to me, or maybe in front of me. I'm not sure which. I pull on the restraints and shake my head.

"You're holding me down with sex straps?" I shriek. *Of course he is.* I've used these a few times. They're something that go under the bed so you can strap your partner down to do all the things they want you to do for them.

Lucas better not do a thing to me.

Or has he already?

I take a quick visual scan of my body. I'm still wearing the same clothes and I relax a little. Not much, though, because he's sitting at the end of the bed watching me like a damn creeper.

"Where is Brody?" I demand.

The asshole ignores me and pulls out a gun, then he slides it up my leg until it reaches between my legs, and he stops. "Told him to go home and be a good boy."

I doubt he would have listened to him.

"I also warned him if he did something stupid, I would kill you." He pauses and looks up at me, the gun remaining between my legs, aimed at my cunt. "Do you think he will do something stupid?"

"Sir." The door opens and a man appears.

I know him.

"Chase, help me." Then it clicks with me what he said. He called him, sir. I've heard him on the phone before call someone sir, and he always stopped to answer those calls. I can feel Lucas' eyes bore into me. When I turn to look at him, I confirm the fact that he's angry. A snarl practically sits permanently on his lips.

"You know him?" Chase's eyes are wide. "Have you fucked him?" Lucas asks.

I remain silent, which makes him angry.

Lucas keeps his eyes on me as he speaks to Chase. "Shut the door and step in." I hear the click of the door and take a deep breath. "Now, tell me…have you fucked my little sugar here before?"

My head spins toward Chase, but the gun between my legs pushes a little harder in and it makes me stop. "You look at me, not him. Do you understand?"

"You have serious fucking issues," I say, baiting him. I probably shouldn't do that considering where I am, but I can't help myself with him, and I'm not sure why.

"Answer. Now," he barks at Chase.

"Yes, sir." Lucas' tongue clicks to the top of his mouth. His eyes stay on me, then the gun between my legs disappears and he lifts it, shoots, not even aiming. I hear a loud thump and I'm too afraid to turn and look.

"You are mine now. No one touches you."

"I am *not* yours." Lucas gets up from the bed and looks to the floor. I follow his gaze and see Chase, dead, in pool of his own blood. "You monster," I scream as he steps over him like he's some sort of shit left on the floor.

"I would strongly suggest you keep your lovers away from me. If you want them to breathe again, that is."

"*I'm not yours, you fucking sociopath!*" I scream out.

My hands clench in tight fists. Who does he think he is? How could he do that?

Lucas walks to the door without a backward glance, leaving me tied to the bed with a dead body to my left.

How the hell did I get myself into this situation?

CHAPTER NINE

LUCAS

"*L*et her go," Joey says to me the next day. He's standing in my bar by himself.

"No."

"I know you have her. I went to her place. Her brother was tight-lipped, but her friend was willing to share. Now, where is she?"

I shrug, unwilling to answer.

"Okay, I'll call Keir and tell him you aren't willing to play." He's always up his damn brother's ass.

"Do you call him to tell him when you take a shit too?" I open the bottle of tequila and pour myself a shot. It's been a while since I've held a woman against her will. "Actually, go ahead and call Keir, maybe he can give me some advice on holding women captive." I cheers to him and take the shot.

"Fucking hell, Lucas, you're holding her

captive? What the fuck? You better not have fucked with her, or else—" Joey snatches the bottle from my hand, and in the next instant I have him pinned against the bar with one hand around his neck and the bottle that was in his hand in my other one.

"It would be wise to not threaten me, *Joey*." I say his name with extra emphasis. He pushes at me, and I let him up and he coughs and shakes his head.

"Clearly, you feel something for this woman. Why do you think Keir took an interest in her?" Joey says, rubbing his neck. "If you ever do that to me again, I'll shoot you."

"No, you won't," I bite out, sitting back down with my bottle of tequila. "Because I would end your life before you even got the chance to raise your gun." Joey and I are close in age. Keir being the eldest, and I respect him for who he is and what he does. But that doesn't mean I'll take shit from his brother. We all grew up together, and at one time, Joey and I may have been considered close.

But time changes people.

Life changes people.

I've discovered I like the darker side of life.

I could have been crucified for my likes and dislikes. But Keir lets me go, knowing that, in the end, I am loyal to him.

He may be the king of the underworld, but I'm the king of these city streets.

"You finished measuring cocks now? Tell me where she is," Joey pushes again. "This isn't me asking, and you know it. Sailor is expecting her tomorrow, and I need to give her the info on where to go."

Sailor is a sweet woman with a vicious mouth who can hold her own against Keir. I've never seen him put in his place the way she can do it.

"I'll bring her to you."

"Soon," Joey warns.

I wave him off and he shakes his head as he leaves.

Damn! I guess it's time to go free my little sugar.

&.

Her eyes are closed when I enter. I step up to the side of the bed and see her jeans are covered in piss. Well, forgot about that now, didn't I.

"I know you're awake," I state, looking her over.

Reaching for her cheek, I stroke it gently. Her skin feels soft to the touch and bare of makeup. Just as I fix my gaze on her lips, she turns quickly and bites my hand until I feel her break the skin.

I go to pull it free, but she clamps down harder, holding on to it as much as she can without breaking her mouthful. I move, not even caring that she could possibly chew my finger off, and climb on top of her, pressing my body down onto hers until she can feel my cock at her entrance through our clothes.

She spits my finger out of her mouth and pins me with a glare that makes my cock twitch.

"You are fucking demented, you know that, right? No normal person would get off on that." I apply more pressure, and she eyes me. "Get the fuck off me."

"If you ask nicely," I reply.

"Get off of me, you sick fuck."

After those sweet words, I do as she says.

"Was that so hard?" I undo the first strap and let go of her wrist, then undo the other. She pulls both wrists down and rubs them before she sits up and looks around, her eyes going to the door, then coming back to me. "You could run, but I'd catch you."

"I'm not your mouse. You can't keep me locked up."

I step closer to her and breathe her in. She stinks, but I can still smell…her. And that aroma is intoxicating. Amazing. Phenomenal. I wonder if I killed her if she would keep her scent. If she pisses me off enough, we may just have to find out.

"Did your mother not hug you enough as a child?" she asks, standing on shaky legs.

"She hugged me all the time. I'm a momma's boy."

Chanel moves toward the door, and I make a clicking sound with my tongue from the other side of the bed. I stay still as she makes her way around the bed to me and we're eye-to-eye.

"You have issues. You are aware of that, right?" she asks.

"I consider it more…advancement. I don't just take anyone into my home." I pick up a stray piece of hair and push it behind her ear.

"This isn't your home."

"No, but I own it." Her mouth opens in surprise, her eyes flicking to Chase, who's still lying on the floor, and then back to me.

I wonder how long she stared at him. *Minutes? Hours?*

"A man like you should be locked up and the key thrown away."

"I don't disagree, but they would have to kill me first, because they sure as shit will never take me alive."

"Lucas…" She leans in, and I lean into her as well, until I feel her breath tickle my ear, "… eat dick and dic, asshole." Then I feel it! Jesus Christ, she knees me in the balls, hard, followed by a kick in the face. When I drop, she knocks me back and reaches for the car keys in my pocket as I cup myself and then she runs out the door.

The sneaky little bitch.

CHAPTER TEN

CHANEL

I run, and it's probably the stupidest thing I have ever done, but I run anyway. He knows where I live, so he can find me, but I needed to get out of that place where he kept me all night. I have to be home where I plan to barricade the door and never leave the damn shower. How dare he leave me like that? In a dank, dark room with the smell of a rotting dead body and my own piss. Lucas is a goddamn animal.

Eventually, in what feels like forever, I make it home and leave his car parked on the street. It's a nice car, probably one of the nicest I will ever get to drive in my life. But, to be honest, I wasn't paying all that much attention to the luxurious details as I sped away to get home. Opening my door, Brody jumps from the couch and gapes at me.

"Chanel."

Quickly, I wave him off and start pushing the couch to the door to barricade it. It probably won't stop him, but it may give me a head start.

Brody helps me manuever it. "Is he coming back for you?"

I stand back once the couch is in place and walk toward the bathroom. "Of course he is," I shout as I step into the shower after stripping off my soiled clothes.

I let the steaming hot water hit me and manage to wash my body before my eyes snap open when the bathroom door is kicked in by fucking Lucas.

That didn't take him long.

Through the glass shower door, I can see Brody run in behind him, but he quickly looks away when he enters the bathroom. "He got in. I couldn't stop him."

"It's fine, Brody. Shut the door."

He hesitates, then does what I ask. I continue on with what I was doing and start lathering shampoo in my hair while Lucas stands there and watches. I'm not going anywhere until I've washed the stench he left me in from my body. And I don't give two fucks that he is standing there watching me either.

"I'll leave, if you kiss me."

Honestly, what the actual fuck!

My gaze flies to his face, and I see a smirk on his lips—beautiful, full, sinister lips. Those lips could tell horror stories, I'm sure.

"Get in, then." I don't think he actually will when I say this, but he surprises me as he steps in, fully clothed, and stands in front of me.

"My cock is sore."

"I'm not kissing your fucking cock better," I point out.

"Figured as much."

I lean forward and, just as he thinks I'm going to kiss his lips, I move to kiss the side of his neck. It was a mistake because when I smell him, and feel his skin under my lips—and believe me, he smells devine—and the way he feels, it makes my lips tingle but I would never tell him that, so I pull back. "Now, leave," I tell him, lifting my hands again to rinse out the shampoo. The water sprays over him, but he acts like he doesn't have a care in the world.

"I should have stipulated where."

"But you didn't, so leave," I bite back. His eyes drop to my bare breasts, and he leans forward. "You can't afford to touch them."

"If Chase can, I can," he replies.

"No, you cannot. Because I set the price for each client. And for a client like you, the price is incredibly high." His lip pulls at the side, when I reach for the conditioner.

Lucas doesn't touch, he just keeps watching.

Eventually, he asks, "What's my price?"

Not being able to help myself, I chuckle at his

words then bite back with, "Your death," with as much venom as I can muster.

Then he steps out of the shower, his black button-up shirt now clinging to him like a second skin. The lines beneath show me just how fit he is underneath it all.

"Joey will come to collect you tomorrow." I'm surprised by his words. "You are working for the boss' wife, so best behavior. I would hate to have to kill you so early." He heads to the door. I'm stunned by his words, but I'm excited to start something new.

"Lucas." He glances back over his shoulder, and I lean through the open glass door to continue, my hair dripping onto the linoleum. "Go… fuck off and die in a damn ditch somewhere."

"See, it's the sweet words like that, that keep me coming back, sugar." He winks before he walks out and shuts the door behind him.

Argh. Stepping out, I dry myself and manage to find my pajamas before I slide them on and walk out to where I find Brody counting money on the couch, which is now back in place.

He looks up at me and smiles.

"Lucas paid me and gave me a bonus for awesome work." He shakes the money in the air.

"You should burn it," I say as I go into our small, dingy kitchen and open the fridge to find it bare.

Shit.

I'm literally starving.

A knock sounds on the door, and I stand there afraid of who or what could be on the other side. Brody looks back at me as he reaches for the knob, and I grab a knife in the kitchen just as he pulls it open.

"From Lucas." I don't see the man behind the voice, but Brody nods and turns to me with a bag in his hand. When he shuts the door, I smell food. Sweet, glorious Italian food. I move around him to lock the door—for all the good it does—then reach for the bag. Inside of it is my shitty cell and some pasta. I love pasta. Carbonara is my weakness.

"How did he know I liked this?" I ask more to myself, not expecting an answer.

"He asked me," Brody replies.

Is this his way of coping with the bad shit he does? Like, here, I'm going to kidnap you, then break into your house when you escape, but it's okay because I'll bring you food after!

Honestly, I want to tell Brody to throw it out, but my stomach says otherwise.

Opening my cell, there are several missed calls. I take the pasta and hand Brody the rest as I head to the counter and sit on a stool. Taking the first bite is magnificent, so much so, I almost want to die from happiness just from eating it.

"Lucas isn't that bad, you know. If you're not on

his bad side." I look over my shoulder to Brody who's watching me, and I shake my head at him in disbelief. I guess all it takes is a good payday to make anyone's moral compass turn gray.

I would know.

I look back down at my cell and call the number that I have missed several times and a deep voice comes over the line.

"Chanel."

"Umm, yes?" I answer, confused.

"This is Joey. I see he let you go and gave you your cell back."

How did he know?

"Yes," is all I can manage to get out.

"Okay. Well, tomorrow, I plan to pick you up at six, so please be ready. We don't like tardiness." Then he hangs up without another word from me.

Really?

Shit.

I have missed calls from clients, but I ignore them—I hope to never go back to that life. Not even if Lucas paid me a million dollars do I plan to fuck him. *Ever.*

"Merci is on her way," Brody says, standing at the door. Just then, Merci appears and smiles when she sees me. Then she rushes over and hugs me from behind.

"That smells amazing, and it's expensive. I've always wanted to try that restaurant." I push the bowl toward her so she can sample the food, and she does, moaning as she chews. Then her eyes soften when she looks at me. "I'm sorry we couldn't help you. We tried."

"I don't think anyone can do much against him," I tell her honestly.

"That's not the point. You would blow up a house if you thought you could help me."

Yes, that's true, I would.

"But you got him out of there, that's the main thing," I say, nodding to Brody.

"He said if we followed, he would come back and slice Brody's throat while he slept. And that he wasn't going to hurt you, just talk to your arrogant ass." She shrugs. "So, did he hurt you?" She leans in, her expression is of concern.

"No, he tied me to a bed and left me." I don't mention the dead body or the fact I pissed myself. I am mortified enough as it is about that little indiscretion.

"But he didn't, you know…"

I know what she's asking.

And again, I don't tell her about anything else.

Instead, I go back to my food, and she tells me about her day.

*J*oey is at my door the next morning, and I open it to him checking his watch. When he looks at me, he nods in approval.

"Should I be dressed a certain way?" I ask, not even knowing what he needs me to do. But they offered me work—work that doesn't involve selling my body—and I'm down with that, even if I'm selling my soul instead.

"What you have on is fine. You'll find Sailor won't care much."

"Is she who I'm working for?" I ask, and he nods.

"She's Keir's wife. She needs help, so he said he would find her someone. She asked months ago, and to say she's getting angry about his lack of willingness to address it would be an understatement." He smiles, and I can't help but smile back at him. He makes you want to smile. I like Joey, he is different from the rest of them.

"I'll just grab my cell," I state, darting back inside. When I turn around after grabbing the phone from the counter, I find Joey has stepped inside and is looking around.

"When did your parents die? How old were you?" he asks.

"I figured you may already know since you seem to know so much."

"I've done a full check on you. You have no priors, your record is clean. How you managed to stay clean doing what you do is…" he trails off but sounds impressed.

"They died just before I turned eighteen," I tell him. "We waited, though, until my eighteenth birthday to report their bodies so I could have custody of Brody." I give him a meaningful look before I ask, "Is that all? Should we go?" He turns and walks out the door, and I give Brody a wave as he sits in his bedroom, then shut the door behind me.

"Sailor doesn't know anything about you," he tells me as we get into the car.

"What does she need help with?"

"Everything you can think of. Just do whatever you can to help her." I nod, not really getting a clear answer, but I know I can wing it when the need arises.

We ride mostly in silence. Joey will ask me an occasional question every now and then, but for the most part we're quiet.

When we finally arrive in the city, he parks at a two-story brownstone and slides out, then comes around to open my door. I get out and follow him up the stairs. When he opens the door, a woman's voice echoes down the hall.

"Wren, you better get back here and eat your breakfast before I call your father."

A little girl with curly dark hair comes running right over, straight into Joey's arms. She grips his face and kisses his cheeks. "Uncle," she says, but in that cute little toddler voice that makes it sound like *funcle*.

"Where is your mom?" he asks, putting her back down. He grips her hand and walks in, then looks back to me. "This way." I follow him inside and shut the front door.

This place is unreal. I don't think I have ever stepped into a house of this magnitude and opulence before in my life.

This is family money.

And a lot of it.

The marble floors are smooth beneath my runners and the pristine white walls are littered with paintings that probably cost more than everything I own combined.

I follow Joey through a living room area and into a large kitchen. A woman wearing an apron reaches for something in the fridge with her back to us. Her eyes light up when she turns, then they darken as her gaze lands on Jocy with who I'm guessing is her daughter. Or maybe she's the maid? I scrunch my eyebrows together not knowing what to do or say.

"How does she always know when you're here?" Her soft voice whines as she shakes her head. "And who is your friend?" she asks, nodding to me.

"This is Chanel. Keir hired her for you." Surprise lines her face as she lifts her eyebrows. She removes the apron, steps out from behind the kitchen counter, and walks toward me. It's then I see she's heavily pregnant.

"Hi, Chanel. I'm Sailor." She holds out her hand with a smile, and I shake it.

"It's nice to meet you. You have a beautiful home."

Her cheeks pinken and she nods. "Yes, I do. It's a little more than I'm used to. But it's nice, right?"

It's better than nice…it's beautiful, exquisite, a dream, really. But I don't share those thoughts. I simply nod instead.

"Joey mentioned you need my help," I say.

"Yes, sooo much. I'm a little flustered if I'm being honest. This pregnancy is kicking my ass more so than my last. I'm tired all day, but there is Wren to contend with and she needs a lot of attention." She looks over her shoulder to where Wren sits on the couch with Joey. "I have people I could ask like her grandmother, but they already do so much for us. So figured if I could get someone to help me around here, that would be amazing." She pauses. "I mean…if you'd like to. I know the boys don't know how to ask, so I just want to make sure you are here willingly."

"I would love to," I tell her honestly.

CHAPTER ELEVEN

LUCAS

*J*oey texted me what time Chanel would be done, so I am sitting out front, waiting. When that time has come and gone and there is no sign of her, I walk up to the door and knock. I hear the laughter before the door is opened by a very pregnant Sailor.

"You still smell as beautiful as ever," I tell her. She is one of the only women, apart from my own mother, that I can stand to be around for long periods. She blushes but lets me in.

"It's good to see you again, Lucas. It's been a while." It has. The last time I saw her was at their wedding. Keir prefers it if I don't come around. "Are you here to take Chanel home?" she asks, glancing back over her shoulder. I spot Chanel seated on the sofa, her legs tucked under her as she watches something on the television.

"Yes."

"Come in. We're having cake first."

"I don't want cake," I tell her.

"Lucky for you, I didn't ask if you want some." She winks and walks away. Chanel turns around when she hears us, her eyes narrowing at the sight of me before she looks away.

"Should I come tomorrow at the same time?" Chanel asks as Sailor sits down.

"Yes, please, that would be amazing," Sailor replies, picking up her plate and eating her cake. They both look at me as I stand there.

"You can leave. I can find my own way home." Her eyes don't find mine.

"That's not going to happen," I respond, my eyes boring into her back.

Wren starts to cry and Chanel gets up. "I'll go see if she's okay."

Sailor nods, clearly relieved.

Chanel brushes by me, careful not to touch me as she goes. I watch her every movement as she walks up the stairs and out of my view.

"Why are you watching her like that?" Sailor asks, bringing my attention back to her.

"Like what?"

"I think you know." I do, but I'm not going to voice it. "She's different, that one. Maybe not quite what you're used to?"

"And what would I be used to exactly, Sailor?"

"Women who are either afraid of you or will do anything you ask."

"You did neither, and you don't see me falling at your feet."

"But you already knew who I belonged to. And no matter how much of a badass you pretend to be, we both know you love Keir."

Chanel reappears. "She's asleep, just wanted her night light on," she relays, coming to a stop next to me. "I'll see you tomorrow, then. Thanks again."

"Of course. See you then."

Chanel grabs her cell and puts it in her back pocket before she walks straight past me to the door without saying a word. When she gets outside, she walks past my car and keeps going.

"Chanel," I warn, but she doesn't stop. "There are a lot of crazies out there." This time she does turn around, but she keeps on walking backward as she speaks.

"*You* are the crazy, Lucas," she says, then spins on her heel and continues down the sidewalk.

❦

Chanel caught a train and then a bus. I watch as the bus lets her off in front of her apartment. She spots me straight away and shakes her head but doesn't stop. I follow her up the stairs until we arrive at her door. She goes to unlock it but pauses and turns to me.

"I don't want to see or be near you. What do you not understand about that?" she asks wearily her shoulders sagging.

"I once slit a woman's throat," I tell her, pausing. "I had fucked her, and as soon as it was over, she tried to get things from me. Information. I knew what she was doing, but you see, she smelled so good, so how could I resist?" Her eyes are on me, listening to every word intently. "That's when the rumors started. I'm not going to lie, I like it rough. A good choking never killed no one." I start to laugh. "Well, apart from that one time." I brush it off, but her eyes go wide. "So, you see, I'm not *all* that bad. I don't kill every woman I take to bed, and I would very much like to have my fill of you."

"That's not going to happen." Chanel shakes her head. "Despite your words…how very touching they are about how you slit the throat of a woman after you fucked her…I don't plan to let you touch me, let alone fuck me."

"You might love it. I can make you love it." I step closer, to smell her.

"Consensual sex is a thing in my world. Even if it's paid for, it's still consensual. With you, it wouldn't be." She stays still, but her nipples harden.

"Why, because I tied you to a bed? You

deserved it for being a smartass. You needed to be taught a lesson."

"Oh, fuck me." She rolls her eyes. "Do you really hear yourself? How fucked-up that sounds coming from your mouth?"

"I've never had an issue getting a woman before," I state. "Until you."

"I feel like that's your issue, not mine. Now goodnight, Lucas." She unlocks the door, steps inside, and goes to shut it, but I stop it with my foot.

"I'll be here tomorrow morning to take you to Keir's."

"No, please don't be. You'll only be wasting your time." She manages to shut the door and slams it in my face. I hear the click of a lock and huff a laugh. As if that will stop me, but I think she knows that already.

❦

I show up the next morning, and she isn't there.

"*D*o you have plans this weekend?" Sailor asks as I fold a basket of clothes. I've been here all week and have managed to miss Lucas at every turn, and I'm thankful for that.

"No," I answer, glancing over at her. She has Wren on her lap while she eats an apple.

"You obviously know what they do." I don't reply, but I don't think she expects me to. "Would you be willing to come away with us this weekend? I'll pay you double." I hesitate. "Lucas doesn't attend anymore, unless he has to."

"What is it?"

"The boys usually meet up once a month at Keir's vacation home and they talk and drink. I'm usually bored and would love the company and help. Lucas hasn't come to the last two, so I doubt he'll come to this one."

"Can I check that my brother will be okay without me?" I ask, picking up the empty basket.

"Of course. He's welcome as well if you want him to come."

"No," I reply, a little too sternly, and she nods as if she gets it.

Walking out, I stop short when I almost run into Keir. I give him a nod and sidestep him as I continue down the hall. He's never home before I leave. This is the first time I've seen him since I've been here.

When I return, I hear them talking and am hesitant to walk back into the room, but then Wren calls my name so I do. Both sets of eyes fall to me as I reach for her. She giggles as I pick her up, and I turn to face them. "I'll just put her to bed."

"Thank you, Chanel," Sailor says and stands, giving kisses to Wren before I take to her room. When we get there, she crawls right into her single bed. Her room is amazing; it's full of pink unicorns and clouds hanging from the ceiling. The kind of room I dreamt of having as a kid.

"Kisses," Wren hums, making a grabby motion with her hand. I lean down and kiss her cheek and wish her goodnight before I turn on her night light and leave. I adore that little girl.

As I descend the stairs, I hear them speaking.

"Chanel." Keir's voice is strong as he calls my name. I find them sitting in the living room next to each other. "My wife mentioned she asked you to come away with us this weekend."

I nod, and Sailor gives me a soft smile from next to her husband.

"I don't need to tell you that no matter what you hear or see this weekend, you do not speak of it."

"Yes, of course. I would never."

"Good." He nods and helps his wife up from the couch. "And have you disclosed to her what your previous job was?" Sailor is now standing next to him and looks confused as her gaze bounces between us.

"I haven't."

"It's best you do." Wren calls out for Keir, and he nods before he makes his way up the stairs to go to her.

"You don't have to tell me what you did, it's not like you were a prostitute or anything." She half laughs, but when I stay silent her eyes go wide. "Well, umm, okay, I really didn't think that one through now, did I?"

"If it's an issue…" I let it hang and look toward the door, already making peace with the fact that I'll be right back to doing that job again by the look on her face.

"No, no, of course not. I guess I'm just shocked.

You just look so…" she pauses, trying to find the right word "… normal."

"Most of us are," I answer, not knowing how to take that comment.

"Sorry, that was rude of me. I mean, I've seen the boys hire prostitutes, and you just don't seem to fit what I've seen, is all."

"Will it be an issue?"

"Of course not. Though, I do wish you'd told me so I didn't sound like a fool just then." She laughs, and I feel relief flooding through me. "I don't judge what you did. Gosh, if I judged, I wouldn't be married to that man upstairs now, would I?" She lets out another laugh, and I guess she's right on that count. It would take a lot to be married to a mafia boss. "Anyway, did you speak to your brother? I'm happy for you to text me if that's easier."

I pull my cell out and see Merci has messaged back—I checked with her, not my brother.

"Yep. Should I be ready by a specific time tomorrow?" I ask her. "Or do you want to give me the address and I can find my way there?"

"Oh, no. No, we'll pick you up. Joey knows where you live."

"Thanks again, Sailor." I grab my purse hanging on the rack and leave, but just as I reach the stairs, the door opens and Keir steps out until he's standing right in front of me.

"I hired you to piss him off," he states. *Well, okay, I wasn't expecting that.* "But you've become helpful to Sailor. So, if he gives you shit, let me know." He retreats back up the stairs. "Be ready at six," he barks at me before shutting the door. I leave, walking out the front door at his words.

"Hello, sugar." I spin around to find Lucas sitting in the dark at the front of Keir and Sailor's house. He looks up the stairs where I stand and places his hands in his pockets. "Trains are down."

"I'll walk."

"Get in my car." Without waiting for my response, he strides back to his car with the air of certainty that I'll listen to him, pissing me off even more. It's been nice not seeing him, but did I really expect that to last long?

I hesitate, because it's a long way to walk. And the bus doesn't reach my neighborhood from here.

"If you touch me, or fucking smell me, I will hit you in the face this time," I warn.

"So violent." He tsks. "Are you sure you aren't made for me?" He holds open the passenger door of his car for me to get in. I slide onto the leather seat, and he closes the door before making his way around to the driver's side. Glancing back to the brownstone I just came out of, Keir is watching us. "Are you hungry?" I swing my head to face him.

"I'm not eating with you. I haven't forgotten what you did." I pull my bag tighter in my lap to cover the reaction my body seems to have being around him, his smell effects me as well. Maybe not the same, but somehow it does.

"I promise not to tie you to a bed again unless you ask me."

I scoff. "That will *never* happen."

"Oh, I think it will." He keeps driving, not sparing me a glance to see my reaction, which is one of awe and frustration at his persistence. "Now, food. What do you feel like?"

"Home," I answer him. "My bed."

"Is that an invitation?"

"Fuck, no." I scrunch my face up at his words while shaking my head. Goddammit, this man does not get the hint!

"You want to fuck instead? Because all I got out of that sentence was 'fuck.'"

"Eat a dick and die," I seethe.

"I hope you don't speak like this to my cousin's kid."

"No, my extra foul mouth is solely and unequivocally reserved for you, which you seem to excel at provoking." I smile mockingly.

"I aim to please." He smiles right back, but his is way too sincere, then pulls up to a fast-food drive-thru and places his order. He looks at me and raises a brow.

"Nuggets," I tell him with a sigh. He orders me a meal, and once we have it, he stops in the parking lot to hand me my food.

"I won't apologize," he states. I stare at his mouth as it wraps around his burger, and he takes a bite.

Why the fuck is that sexy?

And why can I imagine so clearly those lips biting me?

"Okay." I didn't expect him to apologize, so why would that surprise me.

"I did what was necessary."

"Tying me to a bed was *necessary*?" I ask, baffled at his words.

"At the time it was."

"You're fucked-up."

"So you keep telling me. But here you are, in *my* car with the food I bought you."

"I can throw the food out and walk if that's what you want?" I question, holding the food in my hand, winding down the window, ready to do just that.

"No, I'm just pointing it out. You see me as a monster who's going to corrupt your brother, who, might I add, came to me. But here you are...." He pauses, lifts his drink for a sip, then smirks. "I can't be that bad now, can I?" I hate that I feel odly comfortable around him.

"My standards are low, as you can tell." I grab a chicken nugget and put it in my mouth. His eyes are transfixed on me as I bite. It's not sexy, but the way he's staring me down, it's making me feel like it's an incredibly sexual act for him. I look away, not wanting his gaze on me a second longer, even though I know he won't look away because he has absolutely no shame whatsoever. "Do you even care that you killed Chase?" I ask.

It's been playing on my mind.

Repeatedly, over and over again, I watch him die in front of me.

Chase was married, and now…he's dead.

"Not a fucking regret." He smiles and reaches for one of my nuggets before throwing it into his mouth.

"He was married," I state.

"And his wife is living happily and well off now that her cheating husband isn't around anymore."

"Oh, that's funny. How you use the word *cheating* as if it's a bad thing."

"It is." His eyes bore into me. "It's low."

"And killing someone isn't?"

"No. Life comes and goes. One day my life will end, then yours, and so on. It's a natural progression. Sticking your dick into someone while you're committed to someone else is nasty, and they should be buried if they don't have the balls to leave that relationship beforehand."

"Most of my clients come to me because they want things they're too afraid to ask their wives for," I tell him, and his jaw clenches at my words. "And I let them. I let them fuck me into next Sunday. I let them tie me down." I add that last part for his benefit.

His teeth are grinding against each other as he listens to my words.

"Does that make you mad, knowing how I fucked those men? How I fucked Chase?" I almost whisper. Let's face it, he can't kill Chase because he's already dead so I use him as an example.

"If you want to give me the names of those you've fucked, I'd be happy to put them out of their misery." He turns away from me, starts the car, and drives off.

"You can't just go around killing people."

"And why not?" he asks. His hands—strong, sexy hands—clench the wheel and he side-eyes me for a moment. "Do you plan to stop me?"

"I won't tell you any of them, and you won't find them either." I smile.

"I have my ways." He slows down as he gets to my street. When he pulls up at my apartment building, he looks up to my window where the lights are on. Brody doesn't sleep with the lights off, so I know he's home.

"Invite me up?" he asks.

I cough. "Are you asking now?" The shock is now evident on my face by my wide eyes and slightly open mouth.

"Yes. It won't happen often."

I get out of the car and look down at him before

I shut the door. "That's a hard fucking no. Go to your own place and don't come back." I slam the door and throw my hand in the air, giving him a wave. "Thanks for the ride." I practically run up the stairs to reach my door.

Brody is curled up on the couch, asleep with the television on. He wakes when I pour myself a glass of water. "You'll be home by yourself this weekend," I announce. I sit in the chair across from him and that's when his black eye becomes evident.

"Chanel."

"What happened?" I ask.

He shakes his head, not wanting to answer me.

"You need to stop doing stupid shit and think with your fucking head before you end up like our parents," I seethe, then angrily storm off to my room and slam the door going to bed angry. How could he be so silly after everything we have been through.

CHAPTER THIRTEEN

LUCAS

"When are you going to get married?" my mother asks in Italian.

I shake my head, release a huff, then speak to her in English. "Never."

She hits me on the back of the head before walking to the kitchen. "I didn't arrange your marriage like them other boys, so you should be thankful."

Yes, I am, because it's one less person I would have to kill. I couldn't handle being told who I'm meant to marry. Even Keir thought he could do it but that failed, and here he is married to someone picked by him and not his father.

I was the lucky one. My father wasn't as deep into this world as I am. He married my mother in Italy, then moved here when they had me. He worked for

Keir's father up until the day he left my mother, and I only see him when he needs something. It's my mother and Keir's father who are related.

"I want you to be happy," my mother says, putting food in front of me. I try to see her once a week, I'm an only child and I know how lonely she gets. The problem is, my life is busy.

"I am happy, Mama," I tell her, picking at the bacon in front of me. My phone starts ringing and I see Chanel's kid brother's name flash on my screen. "I have to take this. Sorry, Mama."

She waves me off and goes back to making a coffee.

"Yes."

"Sorry, sir. I wasn't sure if you wanted me in today."

"No. Where is your sister?" It's the weekend and I figured she would be home.

"Um..."

"Brody," I warn.

"She went away for the weekend." My back straightens at his words.

"Where? And with whom?" I snap.

"She asked me not to mention it."

"Okay. Well, who did she go with?"

"Her boss."

I hang up and take one last bite of bacon, kissing my mother on the cheek and telling her I'll see her again next week. She asks me to stay, but I can't. I have a feisty little bitch I need to find.

§♠

"*I* was wondering when you were going to arrive." Joey stands out the front, his arms crossed over his chest. "Figured it wouldn't take you long. But, to be honest, I was hoping you wouldn't show up."

"Shit out of luck, then, aren't you?" I look behind him. "Where is she?"

"What's your fascination with her?" he asks. "I've never seen you this interested in a woman before. Let alone someone like her."

"What's that supposed to mean?"

"You have a type," he states.

"What would that be?"

"Prissy bitches you like to dominate."

Well, he isn't wrong. It's always fun bringing a bitch down a notch or two as they so effortlessly fall into my trap.

Chanel, though, this woman intrigues me. And I've never been intrigued or held hostage by someone until her.

I want her.

This much I know.

But in what respect? I have no idea.

I've never once dreamed of settling down with

someone or staying with someone longer than necessary. All those in relationships I see around me, outgrow each other. And I seem to outgrow people quickly. So why waste my time?

"How do you feel that she's a whore?"

"Was," I correct him.

"That's like saying the sky isn't blue. It is what it is, and she *was* a whore."

"I'd watch how you talk about her," I warn, stepping closer to him.

"*Whore*. You want to fuck that whore. Why don't you just pull some cash out and see how far she lets you get? I'm sure for the right amount, she'll happily spread her legs."

It takes two breaths for my fist to connect with his face, then another to watch him drop. As soon as he hits the ground, I kick him in the gut, making him grunt, for good fucking measure.

"Again, watch your fucking mouth."

"You did deserve that," Sailor says calmly. I look up and Chanel is standing there, eyes wide, with Sailor next to her. Sailor turns to Chanel, who can't seem to move or even blink, and says to her, "Why don't you go lie down?"

"I'd rather have a shot." Chanel's eyes leave mine before she walks back into the house.

Joey grunts as he sits up. "I knew it would get a reaction from you." He smirks. "You like her. More than anyone I've ever seen before, apart from your mama." He stands and wipes the blood from his nose. "I better go apologize."

"You'll do no such thing." I reach out to stop him, but when my hand touches his chest, he pushes it away. "Stay the fuck away from her, and me, if you want to continue to breathe," I snarl, as I stomp away.

"I'm your superior," Joey shouts. "You *will* respect me."

Who the fuck even says shit like that?

"When I burry you twelve feet under, maybe. I respect *no* man." I walk into the house and find Chanel in the bar area. She's pouring herself a drink and I sidle up next to her. She pours me one too and slides it across to me.

"Is that all I will ever be? Is that all you people will ever see me as?" she asks in a soft voice.

Chanel doesn't do soft.

Chanel *never* does soft.

"I don't see you that way at all."

Her eyes look up at me with mercy instead of loathing for the first time. "If you weren't such an asshole, I would kiss you right now. But I hate to kiss." She picks up a shot glass and throws it back.

"I'd happily take that kiss, even if you hated everything about it."

"You really do have serious issues. You're wanting something from me I will never give."

"And what is that?" I ask.

"*Me.* You may get pieces of me, but that's all you will ever get." She stands and grabs the bottle. When she gets to the door, she looks back. "I'm about to let you take your first piece. Come on, big boy, let's see what you got."

She doesn't have to ask me twice.

I get up and follow her eagerly to her room.

CHAPTER FOURTEEN

CHANEL

*I*t's probably the worst mistake of my life, but no one has ever defended me like that before, and it switched something inside me. A switch I never thought could be toggled. And that may be an issue, but right now, with a few shots in me and his warm hand touching mine, I'm ready to let him show me how much he wants what he keeps on asking for.

Me.

Just before I get to my room, he pulls my hand and directs me to his. I'd taken notice that it was his room when Sailor was showing me around. Though they did say he usually goes to a hotel to stay, because he prefers his own space.

As soon as we enter, he shuts the door behind me and then pushes me up against the wall. My breathing picks up at his nearness.

What have I gotten myself into?

This is absolutely stupid.

Can someone uttering a few words in my defense really make me want him?

After everything he's done? Because we all know how fucked-up he is.

He's careful when he leans into me. His lips dance across my skin smelling me as he goes, starting from my neck and dragging down until he gets to my dress, which is only held together with buttons up the front. I went swimming earlier, so it was easy to put this on over the top of my swimsuit.

I wonder when he killed last, besides Chase. Does blood coat those strong hands that are now glued to my bare skin? The hand that has mine trapped against the door releases me, then steps back and reaches for something in his pocket. He smirks as he pulls out a pocket knife.

"You are familiar with this." I nod my head, unable to speak, nerves and excitement coat every inch of me. "I've been dreaming about this." He hooks the knife into my dress and, in one swift movement, slides it all the way up, the buttons popping off one by one.

I'm standing before him now in just my string bikini. Lucas moves in closer, keeping the knife in his hand, and leans in to untie the one between my breasts with his mouth as his hands slide down to my hips and do the same with them. I feel the suit bottom drop to the floor and the top gape open. He walks backward to his bed, sits down, and eyes me from his seat.

He's still fully clothed as his gaze burns across my exposed body.

"Come to Daddy."

His words pique my interest. *Did he really just say that?*

When I don't move, he slaps his thigh and I put one foot in front of the other as I make my way toward him. Nerves wrack my body, and I'm never nervous for sex, so this is all very new to me. When I reach him, he nods to my bikini top still dangling from my body. "Remove that."

When I'm completely naked, his hand juts out and reaches for my hip so he can turn me around. "Bend over." I do, until my ass is in his face. That's when I feel his breath at my entrance. He's doing that creepy breathing, sniffing shit again—he's such a fucking weirdo.

I'm sure having a fascination with someone's smell is the strangest shit I have ever come across, and believe me, I have come across some whack jobs in my time. So why, when his tongue reaches out and touches me there, do I jump? He holds me still with a hand to my back as it does it again.

Then, he does the unthinkable and does it again, but this time he doesn't stop. He licks from my pussy to my ass, and I can't help but quiver at the sensation. I'm already wet, my body seeming to enjoy this, and when he's had his taste, he pulls away, slapping my pussy with an open hand. I let out a squeal, and when I turn back around, I find him standing as well.

Right now, my mind is firing with *don't do this*, but my body is not paying any attention. I know this man is fucked-up in all the strangest ways, but his protection in coming to my defense has me thinking perhaps there is another side to him that I haven't taken into consideration.

Is he really all that bad? The answer I know is yes, yet, as conflicted as I am, he seems to have a side to him that won't take no for an answer, and two, there is something there, something unusual but equally as beautiful in his persona.

Yeah, I know, call me crazy, but right now he feels good, and I am going with that.

"Undress me," he commands. I never thought I'd enjoy being a submissive in the bedroom, because I'm so in control of my life. But I'm so wet for him—like next-level wet. And I *never* get wet. A man has not once made me come. One came close once, but that's it, and I always fake it with my clients. I'm an expert at *fake it till you make it*. I'm literally trained in the art of faking how I feel or react to things.

My hands reach out and slowly undo the top button of his black shirt. He doesn't rush me, merely watches me with those dark, woodsy eyes. I have never really taken him all in because every time I'm around him, I want to run in the other direction.

Now I understand why.

He has control, and he's a master at it.

And I'm not one to give up control freely, unless I'm being paid, but even then, I'm still in full control, it's just that the client doesn't realize it.

"What do you see?" he asks.

I've gotten to the second to last button, and as I undo it, I want to step away. His gaze hits me hard, and it's not his normally distant one. This one is trying to assess me, to see me differently, and I don't know if I want him to.

"Your shirt," I reply, knowing full well that is not the answer he's looking for.

His hand covers mine as I reach the last button. "Not in the shirt, in me." His finger touches under my chin and he lifts it so we can make eye contact. "Tell me…what do you see?"

"A man."

He scoffs at my words. "That was too easy, give me something."

"A desperate man," I clarify, and instantly I regret those words when his face changes from calm and somewhat happy to frustrated.

"Desperate," he hisses between his teeth. He bites his lip as he scans my features.

Is this what he did with those women he's killed? Asked them trick questions, then fucked them…then killed them?

"Do you plan to kill me?" I can't help the words from slipping from my mouth.

Lucas' lips turn up in a smirk as he reaches for something in his trousers and pulls out a gun. He brings it to my neck and holds it in place. "Now, why would I do a stupid thing like that?" My breathing has picked up while his nostrils flare, but I don't move an inch. "Interesting." He hums, dragging the gun down my bare body until it reaches the space between my legs. "Do you want me to touch you there?"

I've never actually had head. *Can you believe that?* Most men are selfish lovers, and they pay me so they can be selfish. So when he pushes the barrel of the gun onto my clit, I suck in a deep breath. Then he starts rubbing it back and forth, the movement makes me clench my hands with the friction from the cold metal.

Lucas leans in to kiss me, but I turn my head at the last minute, so he'll kiss my cheek. He doesn't kiss it, though. Instead, he bites my flesh, marking me, then drags his mouth down to my shoulder blade and bites that too.

"Lucas."

"No." He stops, the gun still in place. The

friction is gone, but his mouth hovers over my tits. "You can call me Daddy."

My face scrunches at his words.

He moves the gun ever so slightly, then blows on my nipple, making it peak even more.

"God." I try to push forward to get more from him. How is he making my body so reactive? It must be the shots of alcohol, it's the only reason I can think of.

It has to be.

"If you want more, you have to use your words." He pulls away from me, and my body is suddenly cold, then he blows on my nipple again to tease me.

"Do you plan to hurt me?" I ask another legitimate question, one that is plaguing my mind, but my body is still high from his touch.

"Only when you ask for it."

Fuck, I think I just drooled, and not from my mouth either.

"Daddy." It falls from my lips, and the smirk that pulls on his would make me drop my panties, literally. There is no denying Lucas is a gorgeous man. I don't think I've ever seen a man as good-looking. He has the perfect jaw structure, eyes that could pin you with one glance, and that body? Yes, I'm eagerly waiting to see more of it.

"I'll reward you now." He drops to his knees, puts his face between my legs, and his tongue—the one I hated just weeks ago because of the way he spoke to me—is now doing unholy things to me.

And I love every second of it.

His hands grip my hips, the gun now lying on the floor next to him, as he holds me to his face. He kisses my pussy, like I am something to savor, something delicious, something decadent. I've never had a man go out of their way to please me before.

When I first became a prostitute, I fucked outside of work, but I never got off.

I thought the problem was me.

But, clearly, I am mistaken. Because with just a few moments of him between my legs I can feel something building that I haven't felt before. My legs feel shaky, and my head drops backward as I look up at the ceiling. His tongue works in slow, circular motions around my clit, and one hand moves between my legs as he slides two fingers into my very, very wet pussy.

He makes a humming sound, and I come undone, right there with his face buried in my pussy. I feel him move, but I'm so stuck on that emotion, that feeling, that ecstasy that I can't even fathom saying or doing anything right now.

Is it always this good?

What have I been missing out on?

"That was fucking hot." Lucas stands and my eyes find him. He removes his shirt, displaying a chest completely covered in ink. He's toned, ridges upon ridges and sharp egdes—his body is absolutely perfect in all the ways possible. If you could dream of something perfect, it would be him. My hand lifts to reach out to him, and he flinches back a little at my touch but manages to stay still as my hand lays on his chest.

"What do they mean?" I ask, looking at the tattoos.

He motions to the one in the center. "It's my family crest."

I trace my fingers along it until I get to the lion that covers his arm.

"Most have meaning, but some are there simply because I love the pain."

My hand drops to the one at the waistband of his trousers—a whole bunch of letters.

"Chase's initials will be added soon." My gaze lands on his face again, and I see he's trying to read me. But that's impossible, because apart from the high I'm still experiencing, I don't feel the need to judge. And that's a new feeling for me when it comes to him.

"Who are you?"

He smirks at my words. "As I said, you can call me Daddy right now." He lifts me up and throws me on the bed. I bounce, my tits jiggling, and I manage to lift my head in time to see him taking off his pants.

Well, fuck.

My eyes go wide when I see his cock spring free.

He's big—bigger than Chase and any of my clients. Oh God, I really shouldn't have thought that. But I can't help the giggle that leaves my mouth at the thought.

"Can't say I've ever had a woman giggle after I've undressed."

"It's not because of that." My eyes take in his large cock. "It's nothing, just something that popped into my mind. Don't worry, your cock is huge."

"Do tell…"

"Just that your cock is bigger than Chase's."

The room goes deathly silent, and I immediately regret that I told him. He shakes his head and goes to a suitcase. After sifting around in it, he returns to the bed with a rope in his hand. "It's time to teach you some manners."

What the fuck?

Last time he tied me down, he kept me there all night.

That will not happen again.

I go to get up, but he whacks the edge of the bed hard.

"That is not happening," I say, pointing to the rope. "You clearly can't be trusted with rope and limitations." He looks at it, then back to me.

"If you talk about or even think about another man's cock while I'm near you, you'll be punished even worse. Now, turn around and stick your ass in the air." He drops the rope and I hesitate, then do what he asks, getting on all fours. He touches my bare ass, rubbing it ever so slowly, circling it with his hand before he slaps me, hard, across my pussy. It stings and I yelp in surprise, but then something else happens…

… I like it.

A lot.

"See, there you are. Now, tell me, whose cock are you thinking about?" he asks, then slaps me again.

"Yours," I scream.

"Wrong." He smacks me again. I shake my head, not understanding but I am also incredibly turned on. "Say it."

"Yours, Daddy."

He rubs my ass and leans over my back, his cock near my entrance. "That's my girl." With two hands, he grips me under my arms and flips me over, pulls me until my ass is hanging off the bed, then leans over me, his face now so close to mine. Lucas doesn't kiss my lips, but he starts kissing my body, then goes down again, taking one long lick, before he makes his way back up, paying special attention to my breasts. He sucks them hard, marking me. I haven't had a hickey since I was a teenager. After another moment, he moves again and is hovering above me.

I take a deep breath as I look at him.

This devil, the man they call the viper, is about to fuck me.

And from everything I've heard, he does not have a good track record when he fucks women. So why am I here, with my legs spread, letting him do all the dirty things to me, while calling him Daddy?

"I'm going to fuck you now, and you better scream." He smirks.

That's when I feel him slide into my entrance. I bite my lip as he enters me and have to remember this is pleasure. I'm still wet from where he paid me special attention. It's incredibly tight and I can feel myself gripping his dick, but it feels incredible.

I love it.

Most people would think I already love sex.

I don't.

Actually, most of the time I detested everything about the job.

The problem was, it was something I had to do.

To bring in the money.

But this? How could I ever go back to meaningless, non-orgasmic sex ever again?

He starts moving, and it's a nice rhythm, like he's savoring the moment. No need to rush. He enjoys each and every stroke.

"Let me kiss you," he says, his mouth close to mine. His phone starts ringing but we both pay no attention to it.

"No."

Lucas nips at my chin instead, but keeps moving inside of me. "You'll let me kiss you soon, you mark my words."

I say nothing in reply because his cock hits a magical spot, and my back arches. He runs his hand down between my breasts to my clit where he applies pressure and slowly rubs as he fucks me.

"You better scream, sugar," he whispers so low I almost don't hear him. I'm too lost in my own world to comprehend words. But when he picks up the pace and his hand stays close and continues its circling, I come. And I scream. Loud. My whole body feels like it was overcome with an intense feeling of euphoria. One that I cannot believe I've been missing out on.

Lucas leans forward, his hand coming around my throat as he continues to fuck me. I still feel every inch of him inside me, as he squeezes my throat. My hands grip his to pull them away if need be, but he gives a gentle squeeze and locks his eyes with mine, so I move them away as he comes and everything about it is animalistic. It's as if he is claiming me.

"You're sleeping in my bed tonight."

CHAPTER FIFTEEN

LUCAS

*H*er mouth hangs open at my declaration. I know a few good ways to put that to use. My cock in her mouth, for one.

"If you still want some cock, have at it." I wave my hand at my already hardening cock as she sits up on the bed. I've stepped away to retrieve my cell, as it hasn't stopped ringing.

"You should take that call and leave." She smiles sweetly but I know it's anything but sweet. When I check the screen, it's Sergio.

"Why would I do that when I have you in my bed."

"I'm not sleeping in your damn bed."

"Why not? It's good enough to fuck in but not sleep?" I ask, shooting a text to Sergio, then walking back over. But before I can grab her, she bounces to the other side of the mattress. I step around, but she climbs back on and gets off the other side.

"You want to play a game?" I ask.

"I'm *not* sleeping in your bed," she repeats with more vigor.

"You are."

"I'm not," she argues back.

I crack my neck from side to side, and she tracks my every movement. When I put my hand out to grip the window behind me, she follows that motion, which gives me enough time to jump and capture her leg as she tries to climb to the other side of the bed. It doesn't take me long to pin her down and have her wiggling below me.

"If you keep that up, my cock will soon be back in your pretty little cunt."

Her eyes go wide, and she stills.

"Good girl." I pause and feel her right there, how easy it would be to slip right back into happiness.

I let her hands go but stay on top of her

Easy.

"Now, where are you sleeping?"

"*Not* with *you*," she whispers. Then, before I can do anything, she has something pressed against my head. I feel the barrel and know what it is straight away. "Now, get the fuck off of me."

I move my hand between her legs and feel her wetness. Sliding my finger between her folds, I bring it out and smell as I see my cum between her legs on her thighs.

"Go see a doctor." She hasn't moved the gun away from my skull.

"You smell *sooo* good."

"Good. Now, get off me."

"I could take that gun from you in a second and tie you to this bed in less than five. Which game do you want to play?"

Chanel's eyes go wide, and I move quickly, ducking backward and hitting her palm, making her drop the gun.

"You're going to behave now, right? Or do I need to tie you to the bed again for being a bad girl?"

"So help me God, Lucas, if you do not get off me now, I will never fuck you again," she swears, trying to sit up.

"Fuck! Fine." I climb off because that can't happen. I like the way she smells and tastes way too much to let that ass go any time soon. The second I'm off her, she runs for the door. "Fuck, woman! At least put on some clothes," I tell her as she gets to the door.

She pulls it open and looks back.

"Anyone who sees you naked, I'll put a bullet in."

She steps back in and closes the door.

"Now, clothes."

"You're a real controlling asshole, you know that?" She turns, reaching for her discarded dress, which is ruined.

"No." She throws her hands up as I walk around and open my suitcase and pass her a shirt. "Put that on, then you can leave." She does so, quickly, before she turns and bolts from the room, leaving the door open behind her.

Her bikini is still on the floor and I pick it up, then pad down to her room and knock quietly.

She opens the door, then goes to shut it immediately. "You're naked," she points out.

"Just in case you want me to join you," I tell her, smirking. My cock is hard again just from seeing her, and she glances down at it while I take in the sight of her still in my shirt.

My dick twitches so much—it wants her.

I know, buddy, I want her too.

"Go to bed, Lucas. I'm sure you have things to do other than come here and annoy me."

"Oh my God, Lucas, really?" We both turn to see Sailor with Wren in her arms. She's covered Wren's eyes but shakes her head. Chanel reaches for me and pulls me into her room.

"Tell me when you're gone so I can kick him out," Chanel yells through the door to Sailor. I walk up behind Chanel and press my body against hers, trapping her between me and the door. "Fuck off, Lucas."

"Why?" I groan. "We could fuck here. Anywhere. You pick."

She spins to face me. "I'm tired, and right now I'm wondering if that was a big mistake."

"No, it wasn't," I assure her.

I'm addicted.

And addicted is not something you want me to be.

"Coast is clear," Sailor yells.

Chanel holds the door open and points to the hall. "Out! Please. I need to sleep. *Alone.*" She emphasizes the last word.

"I'll let you sleep tonight, but only so you're ready for my cock tomorrow." I saunter past her and out of the room, and she shuts the door as soon as I'm out. As I get to my door, my head is whipped to one side. When I straighten up to punch whoever that was, I see Keir standing there.

"Walk around naked in my house again with my wife and kid here, I'll fucking kill you."

"Fuck you." I turn to him fully, and he looks down at my naked body, then to where I just came from.

"I put you in charge over there for a reason, Lucas. You're usually business-minded, a little..." He pauses. "Okay, a lot fucked-up, but you do the job without questions." I don't back down as he speaks. "I've killed for less."

"I'd be hard to kill," I argue back.

"Of that I have no doubt. You may be faster than me, maybe even stronger. But when it comes to a gun, I will place the first bullet, have no doubt."

I don't, I have no doubt about it. I could probably take him in everything else, but not his shot. Keir is superb with guns, quite possibly the best shot I have ever seen.

"Now, walk around naked again where my wife can see you, I'll chop it off before I kill you." He turns to leave but pauses and takes a deep breath. "I like her. Don't fuck that up either. Keep this one alive. We need her!"

I laugh as I step into my room and shut the door behind me.

I don't kill everyone.

Only some of them.

Maybe.

Oh goddammit! I know I kill most of them.

Fuck.

CHAPTER SIXTEEN

CHANEL

*E*ven though I locked the door, I felt if he wanted to come in, he would have.

The next morning I get up early and go to prepare some breakfast—Sailor loves her fruits and so does Wren—but as soon as I open my door, so does he. Like he just knows.

"I'm awake. No need to come get me if you want to fuck."

Gosh, what was I thinking last night? I was so stupid.

But, before that, he defended me, and for some reason my insecurities made me act. I don't fully regret it. Despite Lucas being a sociopath, he is amazing in the bedroom. And what's more he gave me my first orgasm, well, actually a couple of firsts. If I had clients like him, I'm not sure I would have quit.

"Chanel, can we chat?" Joey asks as he comes

out of his room, his face a little red from where Lucas clocked him.

"She's busy," Lucas replies, stepping closer to me as my gaze bounces between them.

"I'm about to prepare breakfast. Can you talk while I prepare?" I ask.

"Keir has people for that," Joey says, and I wave him off.

"I like to do it. Keeps me busy."

"I can keep you busy," Lucas declares as his hand slides to my lower back. He lingers for a moment before I remember to brush him off. Contact with him is *not good*.

It should *not* happen.

At all.

"You better watch your words," Lucas warns Joey, and I scrunch my nose up as I turn to him.

"I can look after myself," I tell him.

Joey is silent as he studies us.

Lucas looks down at me, a flash of his tattoo peeking out from under his shirt. When you see him dressed in a suit, you would never think his chest is fully covered in ink. He even has some on his ass. Though I didn't get to investigate the tattoos closely, I saw them.

"Eyes up here, sugar, unless you want me to make you call me Daddy again." My cheeks brighten, and I hear Joey cough and mutter out, "Too much information," as he walks off.

"I'll meet you in the kitchen." But neither of us pay him any attention.

"Do you have daddy issues?" I ask Lucas. He leans in close. I always feel like he wants to test my boundaries, see how close he can get to my lips. I hate that I like him close.

"I have Chanel issues."

I scoff but a smile pulls at my lips at his words. "That seems like a serious problem to have."

"If you say so. Though, I don't seem to mind if I get to taste the sweet-ass juices once in a while. You see, I get addicted." He bites off the last word and leans farther into me, his mouth near my ear, a shiver wracks my body. "And once a man like me becomes addicted, you have nowhere to hide, baby."

"You and all your nicknames," I bark at him.

"Tell me, which suits you best?" he asks, standing back up straight. "Whore is a bit too much?" My eyes go wide at his words and my eyebrows tighten. "*My* whore, that is. Anyone else who calls you that will end up six feet under." That doesn't make me feel any better. "Okay, seems whore is out of the question. How you do feel about sugar?" He's been calling me that for a while, but I still say nothing. "Okay. Baby?" I turn away from him and hear him call out, but I don't turn around. "*Mia per sempre.*" I have no idea what he said, but I'm not hanging around to find out either.

When I get to the kitchen, Joey is at the counter with a coffee in his hand.

"The staff get here soon," he comments, then nods to the coffee area. "It's fresh."

"Thanks." I ignore the coffee and grab the fruit from the fridge and start peeling it.

"So, about last night."

"It's forgotten," I tell him not giving him eye contact, I'm over it. But the words are still seared into my mind.

"I didn't mean for you to hear it. It was for him only. Lucas is…" He pauses. "Lucas doesn't care for anyone but his momma. Never has he shown any positive emotion for another woman, ever. He's fucked some women, then let his men have a go too. So you see, you're different. He gets angry at us over you, and I wanted to test him."

"Test him?" I ask, confused by this conversation.

"To you, he may be one version of Lucas. To us, he is another. The Lucas we know works and works. Keir will never get rid of him. He may be fucked-up, he may have a dark sense of humor, but he's never held interest in anyone like he has for you. And he is loyal, and does what is asked of him, no questions asked."

I stay quiet at his words. Maybe he doesn't ask questions because Lucas doesn't have boundries. He's proven that with me several times, yet here I am.

"He wants you, there is no denying that. I just had to make sure you weren't going to end up in the bottom of some river," he states.

"I can handle myself."

"He tied you to a bed, I heard."

"He did," I say, plating the fruit I cut. "But he also let me go."

"Because I told him to." He pushes off the seat and stands. "I'm second in charge. Keir is our boss. Lucas, though, thinks he's in charge…" He pauses. "In his part of his world, he is. But up here, he is not king."

"Looked like he could take you." I smirk.

"Lucas' father wasn't in with the families as close as what Lucas is. Yes, we're related, but some are closer than others. He used to try to sneak into our house at night. We would go out, and eventually, we would fight. We always throw fists, so last night was nothing new. But it hasn't happened for a long time." Joey walks out and throws over his shoulder, "He won't understand what you are to him. Hopefully, he doesn't realize it too late."

"I'm no whore either," I call out to him.

Joey stops, turning around to face me. "I couldn't care less if you were. I apologize again. It was the only word I could think of that would rile him up, and it worked."

"*P*iper is arriving today. You'll like her," Sailor says, sitting across from me. Keir grunts from his seat and it makes Wren giggle as she sits on my lap, playing with her food.

"She's your cousin, right?" I ask Keir, and he nods, gets up from eating, then walks to his wife. He cups her face and kisses her ever so tenderly on the lips before leaving the room.

"He and Lucas clash because they're both assholes," Sailor states, huffing a laugh. "But Keir respects his business." She looks down at her stomach and rubs it. "Are you okay? I heard Joey talking to you earlier."

"I'm fine. I've heard worse said about me." I smile at her.

"I'm sure you have but know he didn't mean what he said. They just like to rile Lucas up because they love watching him bite." She smirks. "Sooo…" She eyes me and then moves her gaze to Wren on my lap and blushes. "… Daddy?" She can't contain the laugh that bubbles up from her lips. "No judging, but Daddy? Didn't see that one coming at all."

"That makes the two of us."

"But you liked it?" she questions.

I bite the inside of my cheek before I answer her, "Yes, and I wish I didn't."

"Oh, gosh, do I know that feeling." She shakes

her head. "Let me tell you, Keir's and my road was bumpy as shit. Hell, I still can't believe I'm sitting here in this house with this ring on my finger." She holds up her hand. "And his baby in my belly…again."

Wren giggles, then jumps down and runs off.

"It's not easy to love these men. It takes a lot. I want you to remember that. They are dark, fucked-up, and not your average men who stay at home at night. They are hardly around, and when they are, they want to consume you." She glances pointedly at her belly. "Case in point." I laugh at her. "I couldn't fall pregnant before Keir. I thought it was my fault. My ex made me believe it was, but as it turns out it wasn't." She shrugs. "I had what I believed was a *normal* relationship before Keir. Married to a man I thought I loved. But I quickly found out that wasn't my normal. Keir was. Just took me longer to catch up to him is all."

"Why are we talking about falling for stupid men?" a new voice interjects.

I spin around to a girl in red heels who's entered the room.

Sailor gets up and wraps her in her arms. "You have the heels on."

"Umm, of course. Who says no to wearing these beauties?" She pulls back, and I sit there awkwardly, waiting for the introductions.

"This is Chanel. She's my assistant."

"Hi." I offer her a small wave.

"Hey, I'm Piper. I guess you could call me Keir's assistant." She laughs. "But again, why are we talking about stupid men?"

Just behind her, Lucas walks in. He glances at Piper, shakes his head, and beelines in my direction. Once he gets to the table, he pulls out the chair on the opposite side and turns it so it's facing me. Both Sailor and Piper watch us closely. Piper is trying to work it out and Sailor is smiling, while I try to avoid his eyes but it's a hard thing to do.

Lucas' dark eyes are studying me. "You should spend the day with me."

"What the actual fuck?" Piper comments.

Sailor smacks her and tells her to shush.

"I'm not here for you. I'm working." My hands comes to rest in my lap, and I bite the inside of my cheek.

"Sailor." Lucas says her name but doesn't look at her. "You don't need Chanel today, do you?"

"Nope, she's all yours." She smiles at my wide-eyed expression and walks away with Piper, who's whispering to her, undoubtably about Lucas' behavior.

"That was rude," I tell him. "She's my boss."

"Technically, she's mine too." He shrugs. "Who cares."

"I do. Because, unlike you, I need this job."

"I need it too." He smirks. "Now, let's go out for the day."

"No." I cross my arms.

"Ice cream is on the agenda." I squint at him. "Yes, I know your weaknesses, woman. Now, get up and put on some shoes so we can go already."

"You really are annoying."

"So annoying you'll let me between your legs again tonight?" he asks.

"That's a no." I stand and head to my room, leaving him where he is. After I slip on some shoes and grab my cell, I see I got a text from Brody saying Lucas asked what I like, and he told him. Of course, he did. He thinks the sun shines from Lucas' ass.

"Where are we going?" I question as I return to him.

He pockets his cell and nods to the door. "Anywhere and everywhere, baby."

"What did I tell you about nicknames?" I growl at him, rolling my eyes.

"Chanel." He smirks. "Better?"

"Much." I smile, and he holds the keys up.

"Want to drive?"

"No, I don't know this area. I've never left our city."

"Are you shitting me? How the fuck is that even possible?"

"Because we have no money. Why else would I

be selling my soul to men?" His face darkens at my response.

"I hate it when you talk about that." He gets in his car and I follow.

"I don't care if you hate it, it's who I was," I say while doing up the seat belt.

Lucas huffs at me and speeds out of the driveway.

While I have to hold on for dear life.

CHAPTER SEVENTEEN

LUCAS

$\mathcal{M}$y neck cracks from side to side. Chanel sits next to me, staring out the window, and as we come to a stop she sits up straighter.

"Why are we at a private airfield?" she asks.

"I thought you might like to go to Disneyworld for the day." Her eyes go large, and she looks me over.

"You, in Disneyworld?" She can't contain the laugh that bubbles up from inside, and it's magical to see. Her head rolls back and her throat is exposed, her body moving up and down. And all can think about doing is leaning in and kissing my way up to her lips. "This I have to see." She climbs out of the car eagerly, breaking my thoughts of all the things I want to do to her. Brody mentioned it's one place she plans to visit when she has the money. I guess I'll keep that kid around if I can get her to laugh like that again. "Are we really?" she asks again, still not believing what I've said.

"Yes. Do you not want to go?"

She shakes her head and smiles, and it's a real smile, that I know for sure. "I really want to go. But tell me, does this come with a price?"

"Have you heard of the Mile High Club?" She goes to open her mouth and I put up a finger. "Actually, don't answer that."

"I had this one guy…well, let's just say he was a stalker and tried to throw money at me to leave with him," she says as she heads to the tarmac. My back straightens at her words. "I had to put a restraining order on him, and even then, he still found out where I lived and sent me things."

We reach the private plane that's owned by Keir and me. At the plane's entryway, I watch as she takes in everything. She walks over to the bar area and inspects it. "You've gone quiet," she says. "Is it something I said?"

"Why was he a stalker?" I ask. "Maybe he just wanted you and you gave off the wrong impression."

"He paid me to fuck him, Lucas, not to be in a relationship with him. There is a difference."

"Do I need to pay you now?" I ask, stepping closer. "Now that I've fucked you?"

"I didn't let you fuck me because of money." Her voice is quiet. "This is a bad idea. I'm leaving." She turns and heads for the door, but I capture her arm and pull her back to me so her front slams into mine. She places both hands on my chest and sucks in a breath.

"Stay. I've been once, as a kid. It will be good to go again."

"You'll hate it," she states, not pulling away, with her hands still on my chest.

"Probably as much as I hate you," I whisper back. She pulls a small smile as the pilot tells us to take our seats.

Chanel sits and buckles up right across from me. "This is awfully nice of you." She looks around. "I've never been on a plane before."

Then she stares out the window the whole flight.

⚓

They say money can't buy happiness.

I would say, "Have you taken your girl to Disneyworld before?" Because the way she stopped and stared at the castle when we walked in, you would think it was her one and only happy place. Chanel has pulled me to every ride she can get on. We don't have to wait in lines as, well, I know people, and if they know what's good for them they won't make me wait, and by the afternoon we've done almost all of the Magic Kingdom.

"I need one." She buys two and hands me one. She is comfortable around me which I think she hates. "You have to eat it, I've heard it's a must." She bites into her Mickey ice cream and sits on the sidewalk.

I sit next to her, and she turns to me as I take a bite from Mickey's ear—the poor bastard.

"When I was five, before Mom had Brody, she would tell me about this place. That she would take me one day," she gushes. "Of course, it never happened. We never had the money. But I knew one day I would come here. I didn't think you would be here with me, though." She looks me up and down. "You've been a good sport."

"It's only because I want to fuck you on the way back," I tell her, and she chuckles at my words.

"You could have just bought me a bottle of tequila for that."

"Well, fuck."

"Lucas," she says, after a moment of silence. Her next words are a whisper. "Do you plan to kill me when you no longer want me?"

My first reaction is to tell her no, but I can't lie to her. So I stand, pull her up with me, and nod to the shop. "How about a little trinket before we leave?"

"You didn't answer me, Lucas."

"Don't ask questions you don't want to know the answer to, Chanel," I say and walk off.

*L*ucas bought me a diamond necklace, and when I saw the price tag, I walked out. So did he, but not until after he purchased it for me.

Dammit! I don't want to be bought—that isn't what this *thing* between us is.

"I can't accept that," I say, nodding to the piece of jewelry he holds out in front of him as we sit opposite of each other on the plane.

"You can, and you *will*. It doesn't suit me."

"Is this your form of payment?" I ask.

"No, it's a gift. So fucking take it and stop making it out to be like I would pay you to fuck me when we both know I don't need to."

He's right, he doesn't need to.

I turn my face away from him anyway.

But then his fingers touch my face, and he turns

152

me toward him. He wipes a stray tear I didn't even know had leaked and then lowers to his knees. His hand leaves my face and drops down until it reaches between my breasts, then to my skirt. When he gets to the edge of the fabric, he lifts it up until he can see my lace undies.

"I've been walking around, getting sweaty, all day," I say, but that doesn't stop him. He leans in and kisses his way up my thigh to my panties, where he sucks in a breath before he kisses me over them.

"You smell fucking delicious," he responds, then smirks and pulls them to the side. I open my legs wider out of pure pleasure, and not with proper thought. He takes one lick, and that's it. My hands go to his hair and my body sinks farther into the seat as I slide my bottom toward him a little more so he can continue to feast on me.

Lucas chuckles, and I feel the vibrations through my clit, which he is paying special attention to, before he inserts a finger. My hands pull at his hair while he nips at my pussy. I yelp in surprise, but he doesn't stop.

Just as I'm about to come, I pull his head away and push him down onto the floor. He looks up at me in surprise as I climb on top and push him back. A smirk spreads across his face as I unzip his pants, reach for his cock and pull it out, then slide down on it, my head lolling back as it hits me in the perfect spot.

"Sir." I stop suddenly at the steward's voice, but Lucas slaps my ass.

"Fuck off," he snarls at the man, and I hear footsteps retreating before his focus returns to me. "Don't you fucking stop," he growls.

So I don't.

I move my hips again, rocking them back and forth, my clit getting stimulation with each movement. I moan at the pleasure. Pleasure I have never had until him.

Lucas' hand slides up my top to my breast, and he pinches my nipple before his other hand reaches behind my neck and pulls me down. I go, still rocking, my tits now free and in his face. He licks them both, circling them with his tongue, before he takes one in his mouth.

It doesn't take me long to reach the edge. And as soon as I feel it, his hands move to my hips, and he rocks me through it. He keeps on fucking me, even when I no longer have a lick of energy left until he comes.

Why does it still feel so good?

"Say it," he whispers into my ear.

"Daddy," I say quietly, fully lying on his chest now, not moving. He's still wearing his shirt, and I'm sure my sweat and makeup are more than likely going to leave a mark on the black fabric, but I don't care.

"I don't plan to kill you…" he pauses, "… yet."

His words shock me.

So much so, that I scramble up and off him while he lies there, cock out with not a care in the world.

I pull my skirt down and go to the bathroom to clean myself up as much as possible.

I've been in here a while, not wanting to go back out and face him. Not wanting to be with a man who can say things I don't want to hear. Not wanting to be on this plane, or in this fucked-up whatever the fuck it is relationship I am having with this man. It's time for me to reassess where my head is at and get my life together.

"Chanel." His voice comes from the other side of the door. "We're landing and you need to come out and buckle up."

Then he's gone.

Cold Lucas is back.

Why did I fuck him again?

Even after I told myself I wouldn't?

Stupid fucking me.

The car ride was, well, more than a little awkward.

After the best day, he ruined it.

As soon as the car comes to a stop, Lucas locks the door, but I quickly unlock it, get out, and rush to the house. Sailor and Piper spot me when I enter, and they both smile, but their smiles drop when I get closer.

"I want to go home, if that's okay with you?"

"What have you done?" Piper questions Lucas as he enters the room and comes over to me.

"Chanel."

I ignore him and look at Sailor, waiting for her answer. She gives a slight nod, and Piper stands. "I'll drive you."

"Drive you where?" Lucas asks.

I turn to face him, and words go to leave my mouth, but I shut them away and walk past him. I have no energy left. I have no time for this shit. This is what you call the start of a toxic relationship, even if it has mind-blowing sex.

Toxic relationships aren't for everyone, and they sure as shit are *not* for me. I saw my mother go through that with our father, and it ended up killing them both.

"I won't be long." I walk past Lucas and into my room, feeling him follow me every step of the way.

He finally speaks when I start packing things into my old bag. "I wasn't meant to collect you." His words make me pause. *What does that even mean?* "You were his to begin with."

Spinning around, confusion written all over my face as I turn up my nose like there is some awful smell in the room, I look at him and ask, "What on earth are you talking about?"

Lucas shakes his head. "Stay."

"No can do."

"You'll be collected," he says cryptically, then walks off.

Just as I throw my last items in the bag, I turn to find Piper standing at my door.

"You ready?"

I nod and follow her out.

We say our goodbyes to Sailor and Wren. And I don't see Lucas again before we drive off.

"Thanks again for this, you didn't have to."

"It's easy. Though, I must say, I didn't expect Lucas to have his claws in this deep already."

"We aren't…well, we don't—"

"You don't have to say anything. I'm pretty sure everyone in the house is talking about your sex-capades from the other night." She chuckles. "I never figured Lucas to be a daddy type."

"Neither did I, but he sure as shit knows what he's doing."

Piper laughs. "So, this is going to sound bad. And tell me to shut up if you don't want to tell me." She glances at me as she drives. "You were a prostitute? Sailor won't say anything to me about it. She says it's your business, but I really just want to know everything."

"Yep, sure was. What do you want to know?"

"Main question…" She takes a breath and stares at me as she comes to a stop sign. "Did you enjoy it?"

"Never," I tell her truthfully.

"So, you never…"

"Came?" She nods her head. "No. Not once. Until…"

"Lucas," she finishes. "The men in my family have issues, no denying that at all. And it takes a lot to be with them." She stares at me with that look only a person who wants to warn you can give. "Lucas is different, so be warned."

"I know. That's why I'm trying to stay away."

"I doubt he'll let you do that." She chuckles. "He has you in his clutches. Lucas liked to collect things as a kid. He would collect and lock things away. I've heard he does it with people as well."

"Like…collects women?" I ask, confused.

"Yes. He doesn't rape them, if that's what you're worried about, but he sure does know how to push their boundaries."

"He tied me to a bed and pushed his gun between my legs," I tell her. "Clothed. Though, that's not the point."

"Hmm… maybe he's losing his touch. I've heard stories where he takes a woman, then he edges her. And continues to edge her."

"What is edging?" I ask.

"He brings a woman to the point of coming,

then tears it away. And he does it repeatedly until she can't take it anymore."

He didn't do that to me.

Either time.

I came both times.

And I enjoyed it.

"He's a sadist," I say.

"He is. It's why people stay away." Piper pulls onto my street and slows her car down. "Do you feel like he crossed a line when he tied you to that bed?" she asks.

"Yes."

"But you slept with him after anyway?"

I bite my cheek, close my eyes and let out a loud sigh. "Yes."

"Can I ask why?"

"I don't even know, so I can't tell you." I shrug. "Actually, that's a lie. The first time was because he stuck up for me. I was drinking, and for some reason it turned me on…" I pause. "The second was because he did something nice."

"He's collecting you ever so slowly," she states with a tone of finality. "Do you know why they call him the viper?" she asks as we sit in the car outside my building.

"No, why?"

"Because, like a viper, he strikes, then waits until the venom hits before he collects. He is collecting you, and I'm not even sure you're aware of it."

"What will he do once he has me?" I ask.

She shrugs. "From what I heard…the last girl ended up dead."

"That's reassuring." I balk at her words before getting out and reaching back in to grab my bag.

"I have high hopes for you. But to be safe, carry a weapon any time you're near him." I chuckle and thank her before heading inside.

When I get to the door, it's unlocked. Pushing it open, I pause because what I see on the couch has my eyes flinging wide open.

"Brody? Merci?"

Both startle and pull apart at the sound of my voice.

What the actual fuck?

Kissing.

They were kissing.

I can't…

I mean, I can't…

"Merci, what the fuck?"

She stands and runs her hands down her dress.

"He started it." She points to Brody, then runs out of the room.

As soon as she's gone, Brody stands. "What? You knew I always had a crush on her."

"Brody. She's my age," I reply in disbelief.

"I like them older." He smirks. "Don't say anything. I don't judge you for anything, so don't judge us on this."

"Has this happened before?"

"No, that was the first time. But I know she'll be hating herself about you finding out like this. You know how Merci is." He's right, I do know how she is, but what shocks me more is that he knows. "How was your weekend away?" Brody changes the subject. Lucky for him I'm not in the mood to argue, even if that came from left field.

"I went to Disneyworld," I tell him with a smile that I can't help. Even if the day ended terribly, it was a memory I'll have forever.

"Are you joking? Your new boss took you?" He sounds surprised by the tone of his voice and his raised eyebrows that are almost touching his hairline.

"Lucas did," I say, biting my cheek.

"Well, guess we both got something we didn't expect today." He chuckles as he walks away.

Variety
GOSSIP

The City's Bad Boy

A weekend away swirls with rumors.
It seems that where she goes, he follows.
I wonder how long it will last before he finds a new flavor, a
new smell, he becomes fascinated with.
Because we all know it's coming.
Nothing and no one ever lasts long.

"Have you heard from your father?" Keir asks me. We left his house after the weekend, and he asked that I come visit him during the week. He's sitting in his new office, which is not far from where he lives with his family, and waits for me to answer. "Lucas?" he bites out.

"No, I haven't since last year." It's a lie, but I don't want to tell him the truth.

Keir assesses me, like he can taste the deception in the air.

Hell, maybe he can.

"I heard he's gone quiet," Keir states. "Which we know is never a good thing for your father."

"I'm aware."

Where my mother is easy, normal, my father is the exact opposite. He's dark, fucked-up, moody, and generally a bastard. I have a vivid memory of him hiring a prostitute for me when I was fourteen. He'd told me I was a man now and needed to know how to fuck like one.

My father is addicted to sex. He's had issues all his life. Never was he faithful to my mother, and from what I had heard, he liked it rough. So when he deemed me old enough, he made a woman get on her knees and give me a blowjob. I knew what it was, but I had never been touched by a woman before, let alone had one give me head. Then my father instructed me to fuck her, and I was not to leave my room until I did.

I asked her to lie and tell him we'd fucked because I didn't want to do it; I didn't want my first time to be like that. She shook her head, then proceeded to take off all her clothes before she lay on my bed.

Naked.

My cock responded, and she told me to come to her. I only knew what to do from the few pornos I'd watched. After it was done, she was killed, and my father took me to Keir's father, telling him I was a man now and I could work for him. From then on out, my world has never been the same.

I grew accustomed to hookers, love them, actually. They showed me a new world of pleasure. I became…addicted. Then I worked out and grew muscles as I got older. I didn't need to pay for sex. I was attractive and had hit puberty, came into my own.

It was then my father started to resent me. You hear of stories where the mother hates the daughter for her looks, well, my father did that with me. Because he was always attractive growing up, he could reel women in with a simple smile, then would fuck them away.

I don't hate my father for what he did to me, what he turned me into.

Sex and killing—it was all I was taught, and it's what I grew up to think of as normal. So when I fucked a woman and killed her after, it was completely typical for me.

Until Keir became boss.

He showed me that it didn't have to be like that, and that I didn't have to do it that way. I still like to kill, don't get me wrong, but I don't kill my women so much anymore.

I collect them.

And I've collected a few.

Some are still breathing, some not so much.

Focusing back on Keir, I see him watching me.

"You can't kill her…" He looks me square in the eye. "… You're aware of that, right?" he bites out, leaving the topic of my father alone. "She's my employee."

"Why did you hire her?" I ask.

"Because you look at her the way I looked at

Sailor. Like I couldn't work her out, but I wanted to." He glances down at his cell. "Now, tell me you won't kill her."

I push up from the chair and walk to his door. "Goodnight, boss," I say, smirking as I walk out.

"Lucas," he warns.

I laugh at his tone as I walk to my car. As I put the key in the ignition, I hear the click of the safety on a gun and hate the fact I didn't look in the back seat.

"I was actually hoping for the big man, but you'll do," a man says, and I recognize the voice immediately. "Drive, Lucas." I start the car and push on the gas.

"Father," I say while shaking my head.

"Seems Keir wants me dead." My father's voice floats up and into my ears from the back seat. "Heard he has men looking for me."

That makes sense now about why Keir wanted to talk to me about him.

"What did you do?" I ask.

He pulls the gun away, and I look in the rcarvicw mirror to see him relaxing on the back seat, one knee over the other with a smirk on his face. "I may have stolen from him."

"Fuck," I growl, hitting the steering wheel. "You don't steal from Kier. Fuck." I hit the wheel again. "What the fuck were you thinking?"

"I fucking wasn't, obviously. I was low on cash, and I knew where they kept it."

"You knew where they kept it because of me. Do you want me dead as well?" I yell.

"Have you done what I asked?"

I shake my head. "Things have been complicated."

"They always are when women are involved." My father taps my seat, and I pull over. He gets out and looks down at me, the same eyes as mine staring back at me. "I'll get the money," he says. "Keep him off my tail." He pats my shoulder, and I want to lean out and clock him one right in the face. The bastard's a sneaky asshole. Gets away with too much, and I'm always left cleaning up after him. I'm fucking sick of it. "How's your mother?"

I take off, leaving him standing there on the street.

No.

I will not discuss my mother with him.

Never.

Under any circumstances.

That's one topic he is *not* allowed to ask me about. No matter what I do for him—protect him and help him—that topic is off-limits.

I grew up in what I thought was a good household until I hit my teens and realized how fucked-up my father really was.

My mother was fine, she still is—*God only knows how.*

But my father? I hate that I take after him and that I resemble him.

Especially the bad parts

The addictive parts.

It would have been good if I didn't get those predilections.

But I guess not all of us are that lucky.

*W*e're having dinner with everyone for Sailor's birthday. I bring a large arrangement of flowers because I can't afford those flashy shoes with the red heels she likes. When I arrive, Keir lets me in with a simple head nod, and I find Piper and Sailor at the table with two older ladies.

"Chanel, perfect timing. This is Keir's mother, Bianca, and this is Judy, Lucas' mother." Both sets of eyes land on me. I offer them a soft smile and a hello before I walk over to Sailor and hand her the flowers. And try to not think that I am meeting Lucas's mother, who by the way seems normal, and Lucas, is far from normal.

"Oh, gosh, they're beautiful. Thank you so much, but you know you didn't have to spend money on me."

"I wanted to, to thank you again for everything."

She waves me off. "It's Keir and Lucas you should be thanking."

"Oh? What did Lucas do?" Judy asks. She's a short older woman, her silver hair tied back in a bun on top of her head. She has a little round tummy, but she is dressed immaculately in a pant suit and heels, and the clothes she's wearing cover any other bulges she has. Her eyes are similar to Lucas' and are the color of the forest staring back at me.

"Lucas found her, of course. It's how Keir was able to hire her."

Judy, studies me a moment, then offers me a small smile. "Oh, that's nice. Haven't heard of my son doing anything nice for a long, long time, unless it's for his mother, of course," she comments. "Come, you must sit near me."

I glance over to Sailor to see her giving me a soft smile.

Wren runs into my arms, and I pick her up before walking over to where I'm to be seated, as all the boys file in with Piper. Piper heads my way and takes the seat next to me.

I spot Lucas straight away.

He's hard to miss.

Where Keir owns a room, Lucas intimidates it.

"Missed you." Wren's little arms hug me around

my neck. She's usually not allowed to sit on our laps when we eat, but no one has made a move to take her, so I let her stay.

"Thank you all, so much," Sailor gushes.

Keir leans in and kisses her passionately in front of everyone—tongue and all with absolutely no shame or care for who's at the table.

"Okay, well, that's not awkward. I think it's time we eat," Piper comments, reaching for the food in the middle of the table. A drink is placed in front of me and Wren reaches for it, spilling it all down my legs and soaking my jeans.

"This is why I require Wren to *not* be at the table," Keir says, sitting down.

"It's fine. I'm fine." I kiss her little cheek as she hides in my chest. "How about you take my seat while I go clean myself up."

I feel Lucas' eyes tracking my movements, but I don't dare glance his way.

"I have something you can wear. Go to the bathroom, and I'll bring you a pair of shorts," Piper says as she stands up.

Moving my seat back carefully, I get up and excuse myself to the bathroom. I pull my jeans off with some difficulty as they are stuck to me and place them on the counter. The door starts to open and I smile, thinking it's Piper, but *he* ducks in and shuts the door behind him.

"Lucas."

"You've been avoiding me."

"I have a feeling even if I was trying to avoid you, you would find a way to see me."

"Always," he replies, as a knock comes on the door.

Lucas opens it and I hear Piper's voice. "Where is Chanel?" she asks.

Before I can reply, he does and shouts, "Busy," then slams the door in her face, but not before taking the shorts from her.

"That was rude," I tell him.

"I don't care. Now, if you want to wear something over your panties to dinner, tell me why you're avoiding me. You don't want me to fuck you anymore?" He leans in. "For me to bend you over my knee and spank that ass?" His breath tickles my ear and I close my eyes for a second, just listening. There's something about his voice that does things for me—dirty things. "For me to taste that sweet, sweet cunt?"

"How come you never edged me?" I answer his questions with one of my own.

Lucas pulls back, and his brows scrunch as he looks at me. "So you've been talking about me."

I cross my arms over my chest. His eyes drop to my cleavage for a second before they come back to me. "No."

I technically never asked for that info, it was given to me freely, so I am not lying.

"Edging is something that makes a woman come…hard."

"I know what it is."

Thanks to Piper, but again, he doesn't need to know that.

"Then why did you ask why I never did it to you? Because we have some free time and a spare bathroom…" He steps up closer. "Though, you couldn't scream this time with my mother right out there." He licks his lips, and I have to remember to not fall for it. *For him.*

I snatch the shorts out of his grasp and he lets them go easily.

"I take that as a no, then."

"You are correct." I pull them on and smile when I see they fit. "You are so hot and cold. You know that, right?"

"It's only because I'm not quite used to you yet," he replies, surprising me.

"What do you need to get used to?" I ask.

Lucas shakes his head, apparently having enough of this conversation, and walks out. I wash my hands before I head out behind him, and he's now seated in my seat next to his mother. Piper is in his seat, and the only empty seat is next to him. I look for Wren who's on Keir's lap at the other end of the table. For all his hard rules, he sure does break them for himself.

Everyone is eating, so I make my way over and slide out the chair next to Lucas.

"Eat," Lucas orders, not even looking at me, but I know he's talking to me. I ignore him and pull out my cell to check that Brody hasn't messaged when I feel his breath on me. "What on earth would you do with that thing?" he asks, looking at my cell phone.

"My phone?" I ask, confused.

"That's a flip phone. Who even has one of those anymore?" I feel eyes fall on me. "How do you take photos?"

"What do I need photos of?"

He huffs and leans in close. "I have a photo of when you came. I pull my cock to it whenever I feel the need."

My eyes go wide at his words. "You do not."

"Oh, I *sooo* do." He smirks.

I can't believe what he's saying.

It can't be true.

Can it?

No way.

I put my cell away and turn so I'm fully facing him. "Show me," I demand.

Everyone is talking, so I'm hoping no one is paying us much attention.

"If you insist." He reaches for his cell and pulls it out. He opens his photos, there's only one and it's of me.

Me.

Naked, head back, mouth open.

I snatch his cell from his hand and stand, my chair toppling over with my movement.

Everyone quietens and looks at us.

"Chanel. My phone."

I gawk at the picture.

This can't be real.

When did he take this?

How did I not notice him take the photo?

I wasn't that drunk—I simply felt a little buzz.

"I…" I shake my head, and he reaches up to try to grab the cell from me, but I pull it away.

"What's going on?" Keir demands.

I look to him, not even sure what to say, then to Sailor. She seems to read my expression and softens.

"Take the cell to the kitchen, I'm sure there's a charger that will fit," she says, trying to give me an out.

But Lucas isn't having it.

"She's trying to delete my photo," Lucas pipes up, and I whip my head around to give him a warning look. Not that it'll do any good.

"What photo?" Joey asks.

Sailor goes to speak again, but Lucas cuts her off.

"Of Chanel, on the bed."

The room goes silent.

You can hear a pin drop.

Shit.

"Well, fuck. Delete it, then." Piper gets up, and before anyone can stop her, she's standing in front of me.

Lucas reaches for his cell, but I delete the photo before he can grab it.

"Move out of my way, Piper." Lucas' tone is dripping with malice.

"And the deleted folder," Piper states back to me.

What the hell is that?

"You were warned." Before I can even understand what's happening, the cell drops from my hand as a gunshot echoes through the dining room.

"Fucking hell, Lucas! Wren is here," Keir shouts, but I can't look their way because I'm still trying to work out where that gunshot came from.

"Fuck," Piper says.

I step around her to see blood oozing from her arm. "You shot me in the arm!"

"It only grazed you," Lucas says, rolling his eyes.

Piper then pulls out her gun and smirks as she aims at Lucas. "Asshole." Then she shoots.

Everyone's heads drop to the table, and Lucas is shot as well.

"Stop involving yourself in my shit," Lucas growls at her.

Not wasting one second, I spin on my heel and

hurry out of there. Everyone is still at the table, apart from Sailor who has seems to have escaped with Wren.

"Where do you think you're going?"

I don't stop until I get to the door.

But his hand reaches out and grips my arm before I can grasp the handle.

"Let. Me. Go," I say succinctly.

He has his cell in his hand, and his eyes are locked on mine. "You think you can just leave?"

I pull my arm free. "I don't think, I fucking am."

"It's taking a lot in me to not hit you over the head right now and knock you out."

My mouth opens and shuts at his words.

"You are one fucked-up bastard."

"I am. But you knew that before you spread your legs for me. Twice." I gaze down at his arm, the one that was holding me, to see it's bleeding and the blood is dripping onto the floor.

"That was a mistake. One I don't plan to make again." I walk out the door and just when I think I'm clear, his arm wraps around my waist and he pulls me to him.

"I'll be seeing you, *Mia per sempre.*"

"Let me go." I struggle to get free, but somehow even injured he holds me to him. His hand skates along my belly and down between my legs. He grips my pussy, and what makes me so mad is that, despite him being a fucking psycho, my body reacts to his damn touch.

I can't be attracted to this.

I don't want to be attracted to this.

Why can't I be attracted to a normal man—one who would treat me right and not shoot people?

But then a small voice in my head whispers, *Because that's safe, and you only* think *you want safe, when really you want him.*

I try to tell the voice that it's wrong.

It has to be wrong.

Right?

Who could even fall for someone like Lucas?

Does that mean there's something wrong with those people?

To love someone like him.

Not that I love him.

Because I clearly do *not.*

But the way he makes me feel when he touches me, that can't be right.

It's not right.

"I can feel your heart beating out of your chest," Lucas whispers into my skin, his hand moving from my stomach to between my breasts. "Why, oh why, does my close proximity make you feel like that? And we know it's not because you're nervous or scared…"

"Remove your hand, Lucas."

"You are mine."

"Wrong! That statement is fucked-up in so many different ways. *I* am mine. I belong to me. I am *not* yours." I push his hand away and take off once more. When I look back, he's still on the steps, watching me leave.

I don't look back again until I know he can no longer see me. It's then I stop, bending over and placing my hand to my chest as I try to catch my breath. To calm my nerves. To make sense of everything.

What have I done?

I won't do this any longer.

I can't keep on seeing him.

I also have a feeling I won't get much of a choice. Once Lucas wants something, it seems he always gets it.

And he plans to have me.

Of this I have no doubt.

Why? I don't even know the answer to that question yet.

Though, I'm sure I'll find out the hard way.

CHAPTER TWENTY-ONE

LUCAS

"You really had to do that with both our mothers present?" Keir is now on the steps, where I haven't moved since Chanel left. "I should shoot you in the fucking head, teach you a damn lesson. Maybe a piece of metal lodged in your skull might give you some fucking sense."

"Piper already shot me."

"Because you shot her first, dickhead." He shakes his head, and the look he's giving is enough for me to know I have totally and unequivocally fucked him off. "Enough of this bullshit you two have going on. It's making everyone angsty. Fucking… Knock. It. Off. Do I make myself clear!" I roll my eyes and look away because if I show him my disrespect, Keir may very well put a bullet between my eyes.

"Now, are you going to tell me the real reason you're fixated on her, or keep that from me as well?"

He always knows.

Lord knows why I try to keep anything from him.

I always end up telling him.

I hate lies. Despise them, actually.

But I have to lie to him. *Only him.*

And he hasn't killed me yet.

Though, he may this time.

I've kept things from him—things he's asked me directly about.

"There's nothing." There it is again, the lie that slips so easily from my lips as if it were put there by someone else.

Keir walks back up to the door, but I stay right where I am, willing her to come back.

"You better not be lying to me, Lucas."

Then he's gone.

❧

*M*y mother always warned me when I was young to never be like him—my father. *"That is not a man you want to embody,"* she would say. I listened, I did. But as a young man, you can't help but want to be like your father, walk in his shoes, be the man he wants you to be.

My father is a fucked-up motherfucking asshole. There is absolutely no doubt in my mind about that fact.

But then again so am I.

Maybe if I'd listened to my mother, things might have been different.

Maybe.

Or not.

Guess I'll never really know.

One thing I do know for sure, is that I want Chanel. More than I have ever wanted another woman. I'm not sure why, or even what I plan to do with that information yet.

She wasn't factored into my life.

She was forced into it.

"Sir." Brody opens the back door where I can usually be found in the club. He looks at me, and I can see his sister in those eyes. The only difference is her eyes are a little harder, mainly because they've seen more darkness. She's had a completely different life than her brother. "Sorry to bother you, but Marcus asked if we should shut everything down for the night."

"Yes," I answer quickly.

He nods, and before he goes, I hold up my finger. "Where is your sister tonight?"

"I don't know. Last time I saw her, she was getting dressed up to leave."

"Leave?" I ask, wanting him to clarify.

"Yes. She had on what she used to wear."

"You can go now." I wave him off.

"Sir, what do you plan to do with my sister? I know you like her."

"That's *none* of your concern," I bite back.

"I'm just asking because she can be rough. But if you try hard enough, she may let you in. But then again, she may not." He chuckles at his own words, obviously his own mind is waring with what he really thinks.

"That will be all, Brody." He nods again, and this time he disappears out of my office. I pull out my cell and text her, then grab my coat and leave through the back door with full intentions of finding her.

She fucking better not be back on the streets.

Shooting a text off to her, I wait for her to reply. I added my number to her phone under the contact of "Best fuck."

Me: Where are you?

I hate that she doesn't have an iPhone so I can see if she's messaging me back. Maybe I'll buy her one so I can keep track of her.

Chanel: None of your business. Who says you are the 'best fuck.'

She replies quickly to my message, so I shoot her another text while driving.

Me: Chanel…

She sends me back a smiling face made out of punctuation marks, because that's all her shit phone can do.

Me: I'll find you, and when I do…

Chanel: Big boy.

Her words grate on me right through to my bones. I put my cell down and speed until I get to her place. Once I've parked the car, I get out, and take the stairs two at a time until I'm banging on her door rather loudly.

I'm thinking about kicking it down when Merci pops her head out from next door.

"She went out." Merci crosses her arms over her chest in some sort of defiant move, which does nothing but infuriate me more.

"Do you care to tell me where?" I ask sarcastically.

"Depends. How much money you got on you?"

"I could just walk in and put a bullet in your grandmother's head."

"Wow. You're a real asshole."

"So I've been told." I lift my hand to my gun, and she watches my moves.

"Maybe you should watch your cameras more often." She smirks before she ducks into her apartment and shuts the door behind her. I grab some money out of my wallet and throw it where she stood. Lifting my phone, I flick through my security cameras at home and work.

And that's when I see her.

Heels on.

Dress too short.

And I watch her as she walks into my club.

Marcus opens the door for her because Brody's already left.

CHAPTER TWENTY-TWO

CHANEL

*M*arcus gives me a stern look the minute he sets his eyes on me. But make no mistake, I'm not leaving here until I get what I want. I'm sick of Lucas having the upper hand. I grip my cell in my fist, even after I hear it ding, as Marcus tries to shut me out.

"Get lost, Chanel, he isn't here."

"I came to talk to you," I tell him. I've heard whispers that even though Marcus doesn't do Lucas' dirty work like his other men, he runs this bar, and Lucas gives him free rein.

"What on earth could you need to talk to me about?" he questions.

"My brother," I lie.

"And this can't wait until, you know…" His eyes pin mine. "… Lucas is here?"

"No can do." I smile at him, and he shakes his

head as he walks into the bar. I quickly glance at my phone and see a text from Lucus..

Lucas: Where are you?

I clearly changed his name from 'Best fuck.' I wanted to change it to 'Do not answer' or 'Stay the fuck away' but Lucas sufficed… for now.

Me: You should probably enjoy the show. I know how you like to record me without my permission.

I click send and walk in, shutting the door behind me and leaning on it as Marcus stands in front of me.

"What do you want to know?" he asks.

He has a washcloth in one hand and is waiting patiently for me to speak.

I almost feel bad for what I'm about to do.

But I have to do it.

Lucas is keeping something from me.

And from what I heard, Marcus will know.

"Ouch." I bend down and inspect my thigh, lifting up my dress as far as it will go, until you can see a hint of my pussy. "Something bit me, can you look?" His eyes are transfixed on my legs and my pussy. "Marcus, it's stinging," I say, biting my lip.

If there's one thing in this life I know I'm good at, it's men.

I can read a man's expressions and intentions.

Well, maybe not all men because Lucas is a bit of a puzzle. But other than him, I do pretty well. My cell dings in my hand, but I ignore it.

Marcus leans in closer, his face inches from my pussy. I watch as he tests the water, one hand coming to rest on my thigh, his other clenching the rag hard.

That's when I check my phone and smile.

Lucas: I'd tell him to remove his hand, or else.

I glance down at Marcus and see him really looking, his eyes transfixed. Men love to stare at pussy, Lord knows why. I drop my cell on the floor and step back away from him, then turn and bend over to pick it up. I hear his intake of breath, then I stand and look down at him to see if he's getting hard.

"Marcus, I need to ask you some questions." He nods, and I go to the empty table, the one he must have been wiping down, and climb on it, crossing my legs. His eyes track my every movement. "Could you come a little closer?" I inch him closer with a crook of my finger, then I reach into my bra and bring out a condom. "Do you think you can test this and see if it fits you?"

The rag drops from his hands.

He hesitates, but I open my legs just a little more for him to see, and he snatches the condom from my hand and undoes his pants.

I watch as he rolls it on, and as he does, I open my cell to see another message from Lucas.

Lucas: Unless you plan for me to dismember him right in front of your pretty chocolate eyes, I would stop.

Me: That would work, if I were yours. But I'm not.

Lucas: Oh, you are…MINE. Make no mistake.

I put the cell back down and smile at the camera situated on the bar before I look back to Marcus.

"Do you think we can both fit up here?" He nods eagerly and gets up onto the table, his pants now gone and only his cock visible as he sits on his knees in front of my open legs.

I want to say this feels wrong, but sex with men I don't like has become something I'm good at— definitely not something I enjoy.

Not like with *him*.

Fuck him. I flip him the finger aimed at the camera as Marcus moves. I push him back and sit on his lower legs, his cock between us. I lean down on it, giving it a little friction.

"Marcus, can you tell me something?" He nods, his eyes hooded, as he looks down his body at me. I reach between us and stroke his cock through the condom and smile at him. Pulling out my breast, I look up to the camera, and drop my head back. "Marcus, tell me something Lucas has kept from me that only you know." I pump a little slower and look down at him as I grip my nipple, tweaking it.

It does nothing for me.

But for him, I feel his cock twitch in my hand.

He likes it.

"Marcus." My hand pauses when he says nothing. He groans and shakes his head back and forth, like he doesn't want to tell me. I go to move, but his hand shoots out and stops me.

"He sourced your brother. Tracked him down and gave him the job."

What?

What?

I didn't expect that.

I thought…

Hell, did I even ask how Brody got the job?

"Why?" Marcus looks down at his cock, so I touch it again and repeat, "Why?"

"Because of you."

The doors fly open, and we both turn to find Lucas standing there, with a feral look plastered on his face.

Marcus moves lightning-fast, flinging me off of him. My head hits another table as I crash to the floor, the impact causing me to go dizzy for a second before I touch the back of my hair. I feel the slippery blood on my fingers and manage to look up to see that Lucas has Marcus on his knees.

"*Mia per sempre.*"

What does that even mean?

"Let me help you up, Chanel." His hands grip my arm and he pulls me up roughly.

Fury—it's written all over his face. His nostrils are flaring, and his eyes are protruding. Is there a word stronger than furious? Enraged. Raging. Wrathful.

Holy shit! Wrathful is probably right.

Marcus is practically sobbing on the floor.

"You have some nerve. I'll give you that." I pull my hand away from my head and there's bright red blood on my fingers. The sticky substance is covering my skin, pooling on my fingertips. "Ouch," I whimper on a moan.

Lucas' eyes fall to my hand, then dart to Marcus. He walks over and kicks him down off his knees. "You thought you could touch what is mine?" he barks at him.

"I didn't know. I'm sorry, sir."

"Oh, you fucking knew."

Marcus shakes his head.

"Lucas…" I plead his name, but he doesn't look up at me.

He's too angry.

Too fixated on Marcus.

"I wonder, which part did you love the most? Looking at her pussy or her hand touching you?" he asks much too calmly. When his eyes glance at me, they tell a different story, though.

I manage to move forward and Lucas locks eyes with me.

"Did you enjoy it? Because from my angle it looked like you didn't."

I give him no response.

It's better that way.

"I thought so. Seems only I know how to please you, and even now you've fucked that up."

"I fucked up nothing. You did," I bite back, my head now pounding. I start to think this may have been a bad idea, but I know better. This was what I wanted—to find out some truths and I did just that. "You sourced my brother?" I ask, and his head swings to Marcus.

"Your first mistake was opening the door to her. Your second…" he leans down, getting in Marcus' face as he continues, "… was thinking you could touch her." Then, without even a glimpse of

193

hesitation, he puts a bullet straight into his brain. Blood splatters everywhere, hitting my bare legs, and a scream rips from deep inside me as Marcus drops to the floor, blood and brain matter pouring out of the wound.

What did he just do?

How could he do that?

My eyes want to stay glued to the sight in front of me, but I know better. Because if I look at it a second longer, I may just be sick.

"Where do you think you're going?" Hands grab me from behind as I try to make it to the door, my lungs heaving for much-needed oxygen. His breath tickles my ear, and I try to move out of his grasp, but he keeps hold of me.

"Don't you have some questions you want to ask me?" He turns me around, the gun still in his hand, both of us now covered in Marcus' blood.

I look to the floor to see Marcus again and close my eyes to keep myself from vomiting, although my body is reacting strangely, and I'm starting to get hot.

"I thought you'd finished selling yourself. If you need money, you could have asked."

I look back at him, taking a step back like he just slapped me and my mouth falling open in shock.

Hot.

Cold.

Hot.

This man has issues.

Issues I can't help him with.

"I don't need nor want your money," I bite back. "Now, remove your hands, or it will be the last time they ever touch me." My voice sounds even, but it's not. It's shaky, and I don't know what I just said, but it works.

Lucas' hands drop from my body.

"Now, why did you have to go and say that? I enjoy touching you."

I go to speak, but he cuts me off.

"And you enjoy my touches."

"Just because I like something doesn't mean it's good for me."

Lucas' beautiful head drops to the side, the corner of his lips lifting up in a smirk, and I almost forget about what he did. About *everything* he's done. *Almost.*

"You disgust me."

"Not the first time a woman has said that to me, but I do hope you are the last." He steps toward me, but I move and trip straight over Marcus' body. Falling face-first, I manage to put out my hands to stop myself from hitting the floor, but I slip in the blood and brains, still ending up face planting into the floor, my cheek now covered in blood. A scream rips from me as I try to get up, only to slip again and again.

"I would help you, but you insisted I not touch you," he remarks with a smirk.

Pushing up slower this time, my face and chest covered in blood, I look over to Marcus. "This is my fault," I whisper to him, a hiccup leaving me. I bite the inside of my cheek to try to and keep from crying, but I am not sure how successful I will be.

Hands touch my face, and I feel Lucas' thumb stroke over my blood-covered skin, not even caring it's someone else's.

"No, it's mine. I killed him."

"But—"

"No buts." He pauses. "And I'd do it again." He drops my face and I glance at him.

"I don't want to see you again." I rush to say the words, just trying to get them out before I falter.

"Well, we can't have that happen, can we?"

"I hate that you're in my life."

"You don't, not really. You just aren't used to me yet."

"I hope I never will be." Taking a deep breath, I turn and run out the door into the pouring rain. The drops of water cause the blood to run in rivulets over my dress and down my legs onto the dark city street.

I walk as quickly as I can to my car and get in.

As I speed past the bar, I see Lucas standing in the doorway, watching my escape with a small smirk still planted on his lips. It makes me sick.

CHAPTER TWENTY-THREE

J'm sitting behind the bar, staring at a bottle of tequila, when Sergio walks in a few hours later.

"Fuck. Well…" He scratches the back of his head as he looks on at the mess surrounding me. "… You had to go and kill the bartender. Do you know how hard it was to find a decent one to run this place?"

"You have Brody now. Train him up, he'll do well."

"And when he asks what happened to Marcus?" He nods to where Marcus still lies, the blood starting to dry in a perfect circle around his head.

"You tell him I put a bullet in his brain for touching something that's mine."

"Let me guess…" he pauses before he says, "*Her*."

"Ding, ding, ding."

Sergio shakes his head, walks out the back, and returns with a tarp. I watch as he rolls the body up, then drags it out the back before he comes back with bleach and a mop and a dozen other things, I have no idea what they do.

"Do you think me a fool?" I ask.

Sergio stops what he's doing. "Never. I think the opposite." He goes back to mopping.

"She hates me," I tell him, pouring myself a drink.

"You don't understand women," he states. "You are a taker, but you can't take something that doesn't want to be taken, sir."

"She likes the things I do for her."

"In the bedroom only?" he asks, and I nod. "So not in real life."

"I wasn't meant to have her…" I pause, "… to want her. I've had my taste, and I should move on." My fingers tap on the counter. "I should move on, correct?"

Sergio stops again and looks to me. "I don't think you want my answer to that, sir."

"Tell me…there'll be no repercussions for you," I say with honesty.

He takes a deep breath before he speaks again, "I think you should do what you were meant to and move on. She isn't worth it. She'll be considered a weak link. You don't have any of those, aside from your mother. But even then, I feel like you would raise hell for Chanel—"

"Hell's already awake." I smile at him and take another sip. "Carry on." I nod to the mess he's cleaning.

He focuses on his task, leaving me stewing in my own thoughts.

❧

"*T*ell me you didn't," Keir says the next day as he steps into my office.

"I didn't," I reply, having no idea what he's talking about.

"When you request a clean-up crew, they tell me about it. You understand that, correct?" His face is hard. He's pissed off, and his emotions are showing with his sweeping arm gestures. "And have you dealt with Romarc's men, yet? I left that to you, Lucas. *Do not* disappoint me."

"What do you want me to do?"

"I don't give a fuck. Just deal with it." Keir turns away, walking to the door. "I'm sure you have some steam to release. So, fucking release it." He leaves my office in a huff, and Sergio enters along with a few of my men.

"It's time we go and blow some shit up." I stand, and they all look at me and smile.

"Yes, sir."

They weren't hard to find, nothing stupid ever is. Romarc ran a good business, and at one stage, we had him on our side. Then he decided to get cocky, and Keir decided he no longer needed to breathe. So here we stand in front of three men, all on their knees, hands tied behind their backs, as they stare up at us.

"I saw this thing in a movie once…" I stride over to the workbench, spot the drill, and pick it up, "… where they used this. Can anyone guess where and what for?" I ask them, smiling like it's some sort of quiz show and that some lucky shmuck might actually get the answer and a prize.

"That's sick," one of them mutters.

"Wrong." I shoot him in the leg with the gun held in my other hand. I point the gun at the man next to him and wait for him to answer, "Time's ticking," I say, smiling.

"The mouth."

"Ding, ding. I thought when I saw it, *why on earth haven't I done that before?*" I shake my head. "Imagine the drill spinning at full speed in the mouth? Can you just imagine the pain and the fixation someone would have with watching that? Goddamn, why haven't I thought of it before?"

"She made us."

Now those words have me pausing the drill

to look at the last man in line. I step over to him and drop down into a crouch in front of him.

"Who made you do what?" I ask.

"Angela," he responds, looking about ready to piss himself.

I look over my shoulder to Sergio, and he merely shrugs.

"You'll have to elaborate on this, my man." I tap his shoulder, and he looks to where my hand is, then to my eyes.

"Romarc's wife. She wants payback and has taken over his drug running. She wants your boss to pay for killing him."

Standing up, I pull out my cell and call Keir— he answers straight away.

"You'll never guess why they're causing trouble in my part of town," I say to Keir, happier than ever.

"Lucas," he warns.

"Because of *you*."

He's quiet on the other end.

"You fucked his wife, didn't you?" I bite out at him.

"No, she sucked my cock." I hear Sailor gasp and then the cell goes silent for a moment before he comes back. "Pretty sure she sucked your cock too," he adds. "Find her, kill her."

"You sure you don't want one last go at her?"

"You really fucking have issues, Lucas." He hangs up on me.

"Seems our time has come to an end, gentlemen. Thank you for your assistance. I would say it's been a blast, but it really hasn't." I turn and walk out, and the last thing I hear are their screams before the sound of a bullet meets each of their heads.

I wonder what I'll have for dinner tonight.

Pasta?

Pizza?

Maybe something sweet.

Maybe *her*.

CHAPTER TWENTY-FOUR

CHANEL

"*A*re you going to talk to me yet?" Merci asks from my door.

"Probably not," I answer.

"Well, I need to know why you came home covered in blood. Brody is worried."

"I'm sure you helped him with his concerns," I snap.

"That was cruel." She shakes her head and goes to step away.

"I'm sorry. It's all just been so much," I tell her honestly.

"Whose blood?" she asks.

"I can't tell you." And I won't because the fewer people who know anything, the better.

"Okay, well, are you going to work today?" she asks, looking at my clothes scattered all over the place.

"No, I've taken the day off." She doesn't ask why, and I'm thankful. I haven't spoken to Brody yet about what I found out, and I guess now I should. Getting up from my bed, I walk out with Merci next to me and address Brody, "How did you get the job working for Lucas?"

His gaze flicks up to us, then lowers. "I was offered it."

"Where were you?" I dig a little further.

"Walking home from school. A few of my friends knew who he was, but none ever spoke to him. He called me over and then offered me a job." He shrugs.

"How did he know who you were?" I ask.

"No idea. But, Chanel, you shouldn't worry about that. He pays well, and we're doing way better for ourselves now. Aren't you happy with that?" he argues back.

"I'm going to go for a walk," I tell him without answering his question.

I don't know why Lucas would want me, or why he's after me because it's clear he is. You don't just hire someone's brother for no reason. Lucas is a man with a motive, and I have a feeling the only way I'm going to get to that motive is the same way I got it out of Marcus.

Fuck. Poor Marcus.

At least Lucas can't kill himself if I use him.

But is it really using him if I enjoy it? That right there is the dilemma.

Wrapping my arms around my waist, I stop when I see a familiar car parked out front of my building.

"Perfect timing." He smiles.

"Not really, stalking doesn't look good on you."

He turns slowly in a circle, as if to show himself off. "You don't think so?" He raises a brow when he's facing me again.

"No, still doesn't look good." This man is unbelievable.

He walks to the passenger side of the car, opens the door, and nods for me to get in.

"That's a no."

"Get in, Chanel. It's time we talk." I scoff at him and go to head back to my apartment when his voice stops me. "Chanel, get in! And I may think about deleting that photo."

"I deleted it already."

"You did, but you didn't get to the deleted folder in time. Now, what do you say? Will you get in?" He waves to the open door, and because I really want that photo gone, I stalk over and get in. He shuts the door behind me, shoots me a wink as he walks around to his side, then slides in. I think about all the ways I want to kill him.

"Where are we going? I don't have a phone."

"I got you a new one." He places a box with a new iPhone on my lap.

"I don't want one of those. I don't even know how to use it." I try to give it back to him, but he just pushes it back into my hands as he drives.

"Take the damn phone."

"No."

"It's yours. Do as you wish with it."

"Okay." So I roll my window down and throw the box out onto the road.

Lucas slams on his brakes and turns so he's fully facing me. "Did you really just throw a brand-new iPhone out the fucking car window?"

"You told me to do what I want with it. I didn't want it, so…" I shrug.

"Fucking hell, you infuriate me."

"Ditto," I bite back.

Lucas shakes his head and drives off. "You need a new phone."

"No, *you* think I need a new phone. The one I have works perfectly fine."

"Yours is something my grandparents probably had, that's how old it is."

"If you say so." I cross my arms over my chest and sink into the seat. He has the seat warmers on, so my ass is nice and toasty.

It isn't long until he pulls over and gets out. He comes around to my door, opening it and waiting for me. I take my time just to piss him off, looking around and realizing that I don't even know where we are. I don't think I've been in this neighborhood before, but it's not far from where I live. The houses here are a little run down, but not as much as my neighborhood.

"Come on." I get out with a huff, and he shuts the door, locking it before walking down a sidewalk to a single-story house. He glances back at me when he reaches the blue door. "Do you plan to stand out here all day?"

"Depends. Where are we?" I ask.

"My house," he says, pushing the front door open. This is nothing like Keir's house or anything like where I thought Lucas would live. This place has mowed lawns and flower beds. It's old, but it's cute, and it has a front porch with a swing. Glancing at the house next to his, I see it's completely run down, so much so it looks like the outside walls are about to peel off and crumble.

"You live here?" I still haven't moved.

"Yes. Now, stop standing out on the sidewalk and get your ass inside." He walks into his house, and I wonder if it's a smart move to follow him inside. I could be walking into my own death for all I know.

I weigh my options.

I could start walking home, which would *not* be a good idea in this neighborhood. I can walk in *my* area in relative safety because I know most of the people. I wouldn't recommend it if you were a stranger, though. You're more likely to get a gun pulled on you and robbed. Or something far worse.

My other option is to walk into that house and see what the viper has in store for me.

He's already stung me once, and I lived, so what's a second time going to hurt.

Putting one foot in front of the other, I walk to his small porch and step up to the front door. I look at the swing. It appears like it's used because it has a throw rug and a pillow placed neatly on it. I just can't imagine Lucas sitting on it, with his gun in hand, swinging on that seat like some sort of serene scene straight out of suburbia.

"I do use it." His voice pulls me from my thoughts. Lucas is now standing in front of me. "My mother had one when she was young, then we had one when I was growing up. It's what you call a creature comfort. Something I'm used to. Something I like to do when I need to calm myself."

"Do you clean your guns on it?" I ask because that's the picture I have in my head when I imagine him sitting on it.

"No, typically I read."

"You read?" The strained uptick in my voice doesn't do anything to hide my shock.

"Yes, quite a bit."

"Well, color me pink. I did not expect that from your mouth."

"Come in." He steps farther inside and I follow. My feet are met with hardwood floors, which are polished to a brilliant shine. The house, surprisingly, feels warm. Which is odd, because Lucas is anything but warm.

"Do you ever bring people here?" I ask, truly curious to know because if he wants to keep up appearances on the street, then this place should stay a secret. It's the opposite of scary.

It's normal.

Two white two-seater sofas sit in the living room in front of a large television hung on the wall. Under the television is a gigantic fireplace with what looks like an oak mantel. The windows are gorgeous, with their wood sash bars and stained glass at the arch above. A large coffee table with a few books scattered across the surface sits in front of the sofas. The walls are mostly bare, but there are a few paintings scattered around. There are no pictures or photographs anywhere and very little of anything else. Minimalistic would be the word that springs to mind.

"No, you're the first to come to my home."

"Oh, so it's new?"

"No, I've had this house since I moved out of my mom's."

"Not even your parents have been here?"

"Not even them. I go to them if I want to see them."

"So why am I here?" My hands lift to cover my midriff, feeling suddenly sick at a realization, and his eyes catch the movement. "Or is it because you don't expect me to live?"

For all I know, he brought me here to kill me.

"Now, why would you say that?" He turns and heads off behind a wall at the back of the living area. I follow and find it's the kitchen. Now this kitchen's impressive, even if it has that old-world charm. A large oven and range stand in the middle of the huge wood cupboard space. This moves into a breakfast bar where a few white stools with high backs are lined up.

Lucas starts pulling out food and then a knife. I take a step back, but he doesn't seem to notice me as he starts cutting food. When he's heated some pasta in a pot of water, he looks up at me.

"Do you plan to ask me questions? Because now is the time."

"Why am I here?" I spit out the one he still hasn't answered.

"So I can cook for you, obviously."

Huh? He's really hitting me with all the unexpected tonight.

"Why on earth do you want to cook for me?"

Lucas stops cutting and looks at me. "I'm not sure of the answer to that, yet."

"I want to go home."

"After dinner, I'll take you home."

"I've already eaten," I lie.

"No, you haven't. Anyone ever tell you, you're a shit liar?"

"Anyone ever tell you, you're a shit person?" I bite back.

Lucas throws his head back and laughs. It echoes through the house, and I'm amazed by the sound. It sounds so good. How can one person's laughter pull a smile from my lips? He shakes his head and looks at me once more.

"You're good. Really good." He goes back to chopping. "But I already know that. Most people know that about me. I'm not on this earth to please anyone. I'm here to cause havoc and nothing more."

"Don't forget the fucking," I point out, because the man sure does know how to fuck.

"Yes, about that…" He pulls the pasta from the stove and puts it all together in a large bowl. "You should sit, so we can eat." He nods to the large wooden table in the dining room, and I walk over and sit on the white chairs—he seems to have a thing for white. He places the bowl in front of me, then sits next to me.

"Where is yours?" I ask.

"Oh, I'm not having that for dinner tonight." I look to the bowl of delicious-looking pasta, confused.

"Is it laced with poison?"

"Nope." He shakes his head.

"Then, why?"

"Because I plan to have *you* for dinner."

"That's a bit cocky, wouldn't you say?" I bite into the pasta. If I die, I die. I guess we'll see. I try to hold back the moan, but it's pasta, and I love me some good pasta. This is exceptional.

"That's why I plan to fuck you. Because of that sound right there." He gets up and goes back to the kitchen while I finish eating. When I'm done, I find him watching me, his shirt undone, one hand leaning against the kitchen counter.

"I think it's time you lose the clothes," he says boldly.

"I think not. I didn't come here so you could fuck me."

"But you did. You like the way I fuck you." I can't argue with that, because I do like it, very much so. Even though I *think* I got in that car without that thought.

My gaze skims him. I can't help it, he's fascinating to look at.

Why am I attracted to him so much?

Why does he give me butterflies and make me nervous when no other man has ever been able to do that before?

I hate that I have these feelings.

I hate that he does it to me.

I stand and head toward the door, but I don't even make it two steps, when he speaks.

"Chanel." My feet pause, and in my head I'm screaming at them to start moving again. "I plan to slide my tongue over every inch of your body. To taste you. All of you."

Goddammit! Goose bumps litter over my skin.

"That's not going to happen," I tell him.

"You want it to happen, so why lie about it?" he asks. He removes the bowl from the table, leaning down, the necklace he always wears dangles within my view.

"Who said I was lying?" My breathing is heavy. And I hate, *hate*, that I want him to touch me, to slide his hands around my body and do what he just said he wants to do.

Taste me.

I want him to taste me.

Every which way.

His fingers touch the skin on my arms, and he traces them up to my shoulders.

"These do, the little bumps that cover your skin when I touch you. You like it."

"If you say so," I say in a calmer voice than I thought I could manage. His body is now pressed against mine, and I can feel every inch of him. "I can feel you."

A soft, slow smirk touches those sinister lips. "Not that I'm not happy to be near you, but that isn't my cock." He reaches between us and pulls out his gun. Then presses his body back into mine while holding his gun in one hand. "Now, that's my cock." I watch as his eyes darken and the gun goes to the table, then his hands slide under my armpits and he lifts me effortlessly onto the surface as well, lying me on my back where he hovers over my body with his gun in my peripheral.

"It's best you stay still." Lucas moves forward, his lips meet the exposed skin on my stomach, and he places butterfly kisses everywhere, teasing at the edge of my pants before he leaves the elastic and pulls them down ever so slightly.

"And what if I don't," I challenge him, peering down my body as he looks up at me.

"You'll find out when you find out." That's all he gives me before he drags my pants down my hips, taking my underwear with them. I'm now lying half-naked on his table.

Lucas' hands grip my knees and he spreads my legs open wide, baring all of me. I'm not self-conscious, but somehow, my thighs want to come back together, even though I know what he can do with his mouth.

That glorious tongue, which should only be used for this one thing, tastes me. I hear his deep inhale as he breathes me in. Lucas has no shame whatsoever. He doesn't care if you judge him—he literally does not give a fuck. Not many people can say the same thing. Lucas is in a world of his own, and I'm just a visitor.

I want to move, but his command to stay still comes back to me. I don't even know how moving would be possible when I can feel the pleasure rising and rising with each stroke of his tongue.

He's slow, taking his time. He never rushes. It's like he's perfected his technique and he knows with each little movement of my hips what he's doing right. He slips a finger inside me and then another, and I can feel myself reaching that point. My hands try to find something to grip, but there's nothing but the hard tabletop beneath my fingers. I reach for his hair, and as I do, my hips move.

Then he stops.

His fingers, his mouth, completely gone, no longer touching me.

And I was so close.

So fucking close.

I scrub my hands down my face and hear him chuckle, so I look at him only to find he's smirking, his lips wet, and a playful, sinful expression on his face.

"I told you not to move."

"I didn't," I snap.

"Oh, but you did."

I groan and tilt my head back so I'm looking up at the ceiling. Then, suddenly, he's back. His warm mouth on my clit, his finger sliding into me, with slow, delirious licks of pure fucking pleasure, and it doesn't take me long until I feel the build again. And when I do, I try to keep my hips still. I try with all my might, but they arch to meet him, and he takes one last lick before he's gone again.

"This is unfair."

"I'd say so…" He huffs, but this time he hasn't pulled fully away. He's still leaning over me, looking at me.

"Get off of me, then."

Lucas pushes my hips back down to the table, and it's then I realize what he's doing.

He's edging me.

"How would you like me to do the same?" I try to move, but he pins me with one hand to my stomach.

"Be a good girl and stay still."

"Fuck you."

"Oh, I intend to."

Lucas goes back down, and this time, I stay really fucking still, until I can no longer stand it. But he lets me come, and when I do…

Holy mother of God.

My legs quiver, my clit pulsates, my pussy is vibrating, and I want to do it all over again.

"*Mia per sempre.*"

"Hmm," is all I can manage back. *I wonder what that means.* He's said it to me a few times, but I can't work up the strength to ask him. It's probably something along the lines of *I'm going to kill you.* And here I am, thinking maybe it means something romantic.

Romantic with Lucas?

Now that's a laugh.

CHAPTER TWENTY-FIVE

LUCAS

She sits up, her ponytail hanging down her back, and I want to pull it. Hard. Her eyes lock on mine, and I can't help but step closer to her.

What is this woman doing to me?

This is the third time I've been with her, tasted her, and I never want to stop.

But I have to.

We could never work.

People like me can't ever make it work.

We don't get happily ever afters like Keir.

No, we die in a ditch and the world moves on with a care factor of zero that we're gone. There is no saving a soul that is black and tarnished. Ruined. Destroyed beyond repair.

So why am I so pulled to hers?

She isn't clean, we both know that. She may not have blood on her hands, but she isn't a good girl either.

Chanel comes from a dirty family, raising her brother herself, and she did what was necessary. Maybe that's where the attraction comes from. She will do anything necessary to save herself and her family. And I would do the same.

Her hands, so soft and tender, reach for me. When she pulls me to her, she wraps her legs around my waist, locking me to her.

"I think it's your turn, wouldn't you say?" she asks, and I pull at her little excuse for a top and tear it over her head. She lets me without an argument.

I like to know that it's me who makes her come.

I like to know that it's me who can make her quiver.

She manages to stand, her legs leaving my waist, and then she drops to her knees. She reaches for my waistband and pulls my trousers down until my hard cock is in her face. She licks the tip, then spits on it and rubs her hand up and down at a perfect pace.

Fuck.

Fuck.

She does this until my hands grab her hair, and her mouth wraps around me. I don't force her head because I want her to go at her own pace. She doesn't need lessons on how to suck cock, she's had enough experience and does that just fine all by herself.

A humming sound escapes my mouth, and she pulls away, falling to her ass as she looks up at me from the floor.

"Did you like it?" she asks with a coy smile, and I know what she's doing.

She wants to torment me the way I tormented her.

But, baby, I live for this.

My cock strains, and I wait for her to get up. She lifts back to her knees, and her mouth covers me again, taking me all in. Her head moves ever so perfectly and I know I don't need to grip her hair and show her how I like it, because she does it so perfectly.

"*Mia per sempre.*" I groan, and just before I come, I pull her off my cock. She looks up at me with shock, her pretty lips nice and wet and gaping open.

"Get on the fucking table."

"Fuck you," she spits.

When she stands, I grip her neck and squeeze.

"Open your mouth like a good girl." She doesn't. My cock rubs against her skin, and I reach down between us and touch her cunt. She's wet. *Very* wet. I slip a finger in and feel her pulse around me.

She's turned on.

She wants me to fuck her.

She likes the games.

Well, get ready baby, so do I.

I squeeze her throat a little tighter, and she finally obeys, opening her mouth. I keep one hand around her neck, a finger of the other buried deep in her pussy, then I pull it out, put it in my mouth, and taste her.

"Wider." She listens, and I spit in her mouth. Her eyes go wide in shock. "Now give it back."

She goes to swallow, but I stop her.

"I said…give it back." I open my mouth, and she leans in close, careful that her lips aren't touching mine, because we all know she hates to be kissed, and she does as I ordered, spitting back in my mouth. "See? You taste fucking amazing. Every part of your body. There is only one spot left to taste." I release my fingers from her throat and see lust in her eyes before I grip her hips and turn her around, my hand moving to the back of her neck.

"Now, bend over." She does, my hand helping her lean forward. "Hands on your feet." She moves her hands to her feet, and I slide my finger between her pussy lips, then inside. She lets out a soft moan before my fingers move back and into her ass. She tries to straighten, but I keep her in position, and push my finger in and out. The fingers of my other hand push into her cunt, and I fuck her with both my hands.

The moans that leave her mouth are musical. It's like poetry for the sex-crazed.

Leaning forward, I lick her ass, making her moan louder and louder, and I feel her pulse around my fingers before I pull them away.

"Why are you fucking stopping?" She groans and stands. Then she pushes me down until my ass meets the seat and climbs onto my lap. Her hand reaches between us and places my cock at her entrance, then grips the back of the chair when my tip is inside her.

"Sit," I command, but she doesn't. Like a petulant child, she remains hovering over me. "Sit," I tell her again.

"Yes, Daddy." Then, ever so slowly, she drops down, and I smack her ass for being a good girl.

The urge to strangle her and watch the life fall from her eyes is not there with her.

That's the real dilemma with wanting her.

I don't know if I'll be able to let her go.

But I have to.

Her head drops back on a moan, exposing her beautiful throat. As she starts to move, I lean forward, biting and sucking her neck. I want to kiss her, but I know she won't let me, so I get as close to her lips as possible. Just when I think I may be able to kiss her, she turns away, giving me her cheek.

"I'll *never* allow you to do that," she whispers in my ear, riding my cock even harder.

"Those lips will be mine, make no mistake," I threaten.

She has no time to respond as we both come.

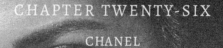

CHAPTER TWENTY-SIX
CHANEL

S hit! I wake in a bed that's not my own. My clothes are gone, and a hand rests possessively on my hip.

"Go back to sleep." Lucas pulls me closer to him. I'm stiff, not sure what's happening. When did we get to the bed, and why am I still naked? "You passed out after we fucked. I carried you in here a few hours ago. Go back to sleep."

"I'm not sleeping with you," I say, trying to move, but he doesn't let up.

"Too late for that," he mumbles into my hair.

"Lucas."

"*Mia per sempre.*"

"What the hell does that even mean, and why do you keep saying it?" I ask, confused and beyond annoyed at myself for letting this happen.

A soft snore leaves him, but his grip

somehow tightens. I pull out from under the weight of his arm and replace myself with a pillow. When I peek at him, he's naked as well. His smooth, muscular ass is on display, and it's really unfair to be that beautiful and so damn homicidal.

Searching the room, I find my things neatly piled onto a chair. I slide my pants on, followed by my shirt. Then when I go to leave, curiosity gets the better of me. While he snores away, I sneak into his closet where his clothes are all neatly hung, but in the corner are photos.

Of me.

Some are from that night at Keir's house, some even more recent. All from times when I was with him.

How did I never notice him taking photos of me?

But the weird part is that next to each photo is a painting, exactly the same as the photo.

"I like to paint you."

I jump at the sound of his voice and spin around to find him in the doorway, still naked. His hard muscles covered in all that inked skin making me swallow, hard.

"You paint?" I question. "Me?"

"I used to paint when I was a kid, but I haven't for years."

I look back at the paintings and they are amazing, so lifelike.

"How is that possible? They're so good." I look back at him. "A little creepy, though."

"You are incredibly inspirational," he mutters, stepping into the small space until he's standing next to me. He opens a cabinet and I glance inside, immediately wishing I hadn't.

Pictures of other women line the cupboard.

"Did you paint them as well?" I ask.

He picks up the first one and shows it to me. "This one liked to be choked until she passed out and demanded that I keep fucking her, so when she woke, she came."

I stare at him, not knowing what else to do because I certainly have nothing to say.

"I killed her." He shrugs, like it wasn't a big deal.

He pulls out another. "This one...she was quiet, shy to begin with. Until she got in the bedroom. Then her freak flag flew." He pauses, dropping it. "I killed her too." He looks at me now.

"Why?" I ask on a breath, feeling heat rising into my chest at his admissions. *Why would he do that?*

"I like to watch the life leave their eyes while I fuck them, and I didn't like the way they smelled anymore."

"What did they smell like?"

"Betrayal," he remarks in a voice that sends shivers over me, and my brows quickly squish together. My end looking a lot closer than I was anticipating.

"Do you plan to add me to your collection?" I nod to the cabinet. There are multiple photos of some of the women, but others just have one.

"No," he answers simply. "Now, how about some food?" He turns around without another word, walks out, and leaves me in his closet, with too much to think about.

"If you really want to find the good stuff, open the cupboard on the top in the wardrobe." He chuckles, and I turn, looking up to the only one with a handle, and I reach for it. My hand pauses, wondering if this is a good idea or an incredibly stupid one.

Biting my inner cheek, I do it anyway. Inside, I find a box. Pulling it down and opening it, there are whips, handcuffs, dildos, and other devices I could never name, as well as photos of naked women, dead. Quickly putting it back, I hurry out to find him at the kitchen counter, making coffee.

"I need to go home," I tell him.

"I'll drive you. Or you can just stay?" he asks.

"No, I need to go home. Now." I should be running out the door after what I just saw and what he told me. Yet, my feet remain plastered to the floor. *Why?*

Is what Sailor said true? That it takes someone different to be able to want to be with someone like him? Am I different or just a little fucked-up? I'm not even sure anymore. And those photos, that's not normal, this is not normal.

"Thanks for the, um…sex." I offer him a wave and make my way to the front door. I step out onto the porch and find him right behind me, still naked. I look around and see people walking about, but he has not a care in the world.

"Take these." He throws something at me, and I just manage to catch it. It's the keys to his car. "You remember how to drive, right? From the last time you stole it from me?"

I nod, speechless.

"Good. Because I plan to go back to bed. And if you won't join me—"

"I won't," I cut him off, going to hand him the keys. I don't want anything of his.

"I'll be seeing you, *Mia per sempre*." He goes back inside, shutting the door behind him. I walk to his car, which is still parked out front, and climb inside.

My hands rub the steering wheel and I like the way the leather feels.

Glancing at the house, I see no sign of him as I leave.

*ell, fuck.*

Where is the car?

I parked it here a few hours ago, but when I came back out to check on it—*because hello, shit neighborhood*—it was gone.

Biting my cheek, I taste my own blood.

How do I tell him his car's been stolen?

From my place.

Will he be mad?

I'm not sure I want to see him angry. I've seen him furious at others, but never at me.

Walking back inside, I find his number and press call and he answers, sounding half asleep. "Chanel." He says my name when I don't speak.

"So…" I begin, but the rest of the words don't want to leave my mouth. "Did you pick up your car?"

"No," he replies, and I can hear him waking up a little more. "Is my car not with you?"

"I *may* have misplaced it." I groan, banging my head on the wall.

"It's hard to misplace a car," he comments, but his tone gives nothing away. He doesn't sound upset with me like I thought he would be. "Hold on."

"What are you doing?"

"I'm tracking it." A sigh leaves me as I hear a few things clicking and then he swears. "You'll make this up to me."

"It wasn't my fault," I tell him, but stop myself from saying any more since that isn't exactly true. I could have just stayed with him and this wouldn't have happened. Or, at least, that would be his reasoning. He stays quiet, and I reluctantly ask, "Fine, what do you want?"

"You can take the new phone I bought you. And, Chanel, if you throw this one out, I will spank your ass."

"This was your plan all along," I accuse.

"Yeah, I totally planned for my car to be stolen."

"Are you going to get it back?" I ask. "Can I come?"

"You want to come to get my car?" he asks, sounding genuinely surprised.

"Yes, if that's okay."

"Sergio is on his way to collect you." He hangs up.

Running inside, I slide on some jeans and throw on a baggy shirt after I pull off my nighty. When I walk out of my room, Brody's sitting on the couch playing his Xbox.

"You off?" he calls out, and I just nod and walk out the door.

Sergio is pulling up to the curb when I shut the door behind me. I climb into the front seat and offer him a warm smile. "Hi." He doesn't reply, just drives to Lucas' place in complete silence.

Lucas approaches the car, typing away on his cell, not paying us any attention.

"Get in the back," Sergio says to me, and Lucas looks up.

"She can stay where she is if she wants."

I undo my seat belt and climb into the back. Surprisingly, Lucas gets in the back with me, and he only puts his cell down once we're moving.

"Did you sleep?"

I nod. I tried, but I didn't get far. All my thoughts were of his hands roaming my body in every which way possible. I'm clearly not telling him that, though.

"You would have slept better in my bed."

"With photos of all your other women? That's a hard no." I shake my head, and he reaches into the back pocket of the seat in front of him, then passes me an iPhone box.

"One more time. I *will* spank your ass." I take it from his hand and glance to the window. "Chanel," he warns, and I can't help the chuckle that bubbles up from inside me.

"Calm down, I'm not throwing it out." I open the box and am met with a light blue iPhone.

"I've seen you wear that color."

I'm surprised he remembers. I feel him watching me, so I turn toward him. "Thank you."

"That thing you call a phone can't do anything but call."

"It can text."

"*It can text*," he mimics me with a shake of his head. "It's a piece of shit. There is another in that pocket." He nods toward it. "For your brother."

"You don't need to buy us," I tell him. "I'm not for sale anymore."

"It's a gift, Chanel. For fuck's sake, take it."

I huff as we keep driving. "Where are we going?" I ask. Instead of answering, he takes the cell from my grasp and then makes a grabby hand motion in front of my face. I have no idea what he means, so I sit there, confused with a raised brow.

"Give me your old cell." I reach into my pocket and give him my phone. He exhales a soft laugh as he turns it around and pulls the sim card out. "You'll have to change your number, this sim card won't work." He gives me my phone back and then turns on the other and sets it up. "Email." I rattle off my email, and when he's done entering it, he looks at me. "Lean in." I'm confused why he would want me to do that, but I do it anyway. Leaning in close to me, he lifts the cell and then snaps a photo.

"What did you do that for?"

"So you can remember who you belong to."

"I belong to me, Lucas," I say back to him, my eyes locked on his.

"Wrong. You. Are. Mine. And if you think any other man will be touching you, think again. I'll tear him limb from limb and make you watch." He smirks, then hands me my cell phone back.

"You're all kinds of fucked-up."

"Why, thank you. The compliments you keep throwing at me do so much for my ego."

"I'm sure you don't need that ego stroked in the least. I'm sure you do that enough yourself."

Sergio coughs from the front seat, and I see him trying to hide his smile.

"This may be true, but I do enjoy keeping you around."

"How nice. Did you enjoy keeping around the other women too?" I tease him.

"No, just you."

"I can officially die a happy woman that I, a hooker from a shit neighborhood, has caught your eye and kept it…" I pause for dramatic effect, "… for the time being. How *lucky* am I."

"Don't call yourself that," he commands.

"What? A hooker?" I ask. "I was. Or have you conveniently forgotten?"

"I have not. Your past seems to remind me, though."

"What's that meant to mean?" I ask.

"Nothing," he snaps.

And his whole demeanor changes.

He's now angry.

At me?

CHAPTER TWENTY-SEVEN

LUCAS

We pull up to the house and I see my car sitting out front. Sergio shakes his head when he realizes whose house it is. Chanel gets out and walks around the car until she's next to me.

"Did they want you to find it?" she asks, confused. "It's just sitting there, parked in the driveway." The all-white house and the empty yard make it look like no one is home as the lights are off, but we know better. I enter through the gate with Chanel behind me and stalk up to the door, knocking three times with force.

The door opens, and there she stands.

"Angela." She bites her bottom lip and then glances at Chanel. Her nose lifts in disgust before she opens the door for me to walk in.

"Just you," she says.

"You don't get to call the shots here, you know that." I grab Chanel by the hand and walk her in with me, with Sergio following closely behind. Angela leads us to her living room, and she sits on one of the sofas, picking up her glass of red wine.

"I would offer you one, but I'm sure this isn't a social call."

"You are correct, this is far from social." I can feel Chanel's eyes on me, but I keep my focus on Angela. "So—"

"You never called me back," she interrupts. "I had to get your attention somehow." Chanel tenses next to me. "You obviously know what a good lover this man is, correct?" Angela's eyes are on Chanel, but Chanel gives her nothing in return.

Smart girl.

"Angela, you suck cock. It's what you're good at." Her eyes flare, and she squeezes the glass in her hand a little tighter. "Don't try to tell yourself otherwise. You sucked Keir's, then you came to me. Who's next?"

"I should have lit your car on fire," she remarks, her knuckles turning white.

"That would have been a bad move. I would have come in and killed you immediately."

"Fuck you," she spits.

"Again, you've tried that. Are you that lonely without your worthless piece of shit of a husband here anymore?" Keir killed her husband for betraying him, but it wasn't the betrayal that pushed Keir over the edge to kill him. It was the fact that one night at a club, Romarc had gone up to Sailor and spoke to her.

That was Keir's breaking point.

Romarc also thought he could kidnap Keir's bitch of an arranged fiancée, Paige. But again, he didn't care until Romarc came near Sailor. Then all bets were off.

"You know he's mad at you," I inform her, referring to Keir.

"He can fuck off."

"Now, now…don't get your knickers in a twist." I shake my head slightly. "You know if he walked up those stairs and was at your door, you would take him in a heartbeat."

"You killed my men," she screams at me.

"Why were you making trouble, Angela? Did you want me here? Or maybe it was Keir you wanted here."

She stands, throwing her wine at my face. "I hate you."

"I feel like all the ladies say that to him," Chanel pipes in, it's quiet but everyone heard the words. I turn to face her and see her shrugging. "What? It's true. Do you have any friends?"

"You're my friend."

"Lies. I am not."

"Okay, well, you like it when I fuck you." I hear

heels clacking away from us as I stare at her. *How can she mesmerize me so much?* She bites her cheek, and I lift my hand to touch her lip. "Stop biting yourself." Her cheek pops out and she looks at me as if she's truly seeing me. "You do it when you're nervous or lost in thought."

"I fuck you out of pity," she states after I feel her take a breath, but it doesn't come out as fiercely as she wants it to.

My finger touches her lip and pulls it down. "Did that lie taste sour leaving your lips?" I lean in, and she holds still.

"Not as sour as the lies that leak from yours."

We both know *that's* a lie.

We both hear the click of a gun and turn to find Angela standing behind us, gun ready and aimed in hand. She doesn't have it pointed at me, though. No, it's pointed at Chanel.

"Angela…"

"I see the way you look at her. It's the way Keir looks at Sailor. I see it. Romarc never looked at me like that. He and all his harlots. I want someone to want me the way you want her." She pauses, glancing at me. "You would kill for her."

"I would," I agree without a doubt. But what she doesn't know is we all have our weak spots. Chanel may be one of mine, but not the only one. "If you don't drop it."

"You'll what? Kill me? Keir never did, so why

would you?" She drops her head to the side, then glances back at Chanel. I see her finger twitch, and just before she can pull the trigger, I reach for the gun and grip it. While she's distracted with trying to wrestle the gun back, I shoot her in the stomach. But I am too late. In the struggle, her finger was able to squeeze the trigger and her gun went off.

My frantic gaze searches out Chanel, and I see her eyes wide as she stands there covered in blood before she falls to the floor.

"Where?" I grab for her to help lay her down, but she just stares at me. "Chanel. Where are you hurt?" I ask her again as my eyes scan her from top to bottom.

"I…"

Sergio is keeping an eye on Angela. He speaks to me in Italian, asking me if he can end her life.

"*Finiscilo,*" I tell him to finish it.

Chanel's eyes lock on mine, and I want to lean in, but first, I reach for her shirt and lift it up to check for wounds. There's nothing on her stomach. "You're not hurt?"

"You shot her in front of me. Like she was nothing." Her brows pull together. "Again." *Now she's mad.* "The next time you kill someone in front of me, I will knee you in the balls so fucking hard you won't know which way is up." The fire is back in her eyes. "I'm sick of being covered in blood when I am around you. Sick of it, you hear me?"

She stands and glares down at Angela. "Think the crazy bitch would mind if I used her shower?" I look down at Angela to find her gone, her eyes wide open but they're unseeing.

"No," I say, standing to follow her.

"Don't even fucking think about it." She stomps off and up the stairs to what I guess are the main rooms. I hear a door slam before I look away.

"Keir is going to be pissed," Sergio remarks.

"No, he won't. He basically told me to do this."

"Did he say to fix it?"

"Is that not what I did?" I question.

"Looks to me like you killed her, not so much… you know, fixed it."

"Yeah, yeah. Semantics." I make my way to the stairs.

"If she knees you in the balls, should I call an ambulance?" Sergio laughs.

"You'd be best calling the morgue with what I'm about to do to her."

"You are so lost," I hear Sergio mutter as I make my way up the stairs.

Her clothes are lying on the floor, meaning she must have torn them off as she walked up. The water is running as I make my way into the bathroom. Her back is to me, and her head is under the water as she washes her soft, long locks.

"I think you should touch yourself," I tell her.

She groans loudly. "You really don't listen to a

word I say, do you?" But her hand moves like on autopilot to her breast at my words.

"No, but did you expect any less?" I sit on the closed toilet seat as she turns to face me, her body on full display. The more things I plan to do to that body, I can only imagine.

"I guess not."

"Now, if you would be so kind…touch yourself."

"How about *no*?" she answers, but her hand moves anyway. She rubs her breasts before she drops her hand between her legs and starts moving, and my cock strains against my pants.

"Now, tell me, how much do you want me to bend you over right now and take your sweet-ass pussy into my mouth and have it for lunch, dinner, and dessert?" She presses herself up against the shower door, the steam coating the glass, her breasts now squashed against it and her hand just visible as she rubs her clit.

"*Mia per sempre.*"

"Yes," she says on a moan, and I see her head lolling back—it's what she does when she's close.

"See, you like the way I speak to you. The way I touch you." I stand and approach the shower, and her eyes pop open. "Remember that when I bring you back to mine tonight to fuck some better manners into you."

I walk out and hear her groan as I leave.

CHAPTER TWENTY-EIGHT

CHANEL

*Q*uickly, I wrap a towel around me as I get out of the shower. Lucas is sitting on her bed, cell in hand, when I exit the bathroom.

"What are you doing?"

"Playing *Clash of Clans*." Umm, okay, whatever that is. "Clothes are in the dresser." He nods, then goes back to his cell. I open the drawer and pull out a dress. When I see the brand, I quickly shove it back inside and close the drawer.

"All her shit is going to be designer, just pick something so we can go."

I turn to see him still on his cell, whatever he's doing his interest is not wavering, so I do what any woman would.

"Don't pull that face at me either." He looks up

to confirm I was pulling a face of annoyance at him.

"I don't wear this shit."

"Feel free to put on your old stuff then if it's an issue."

"My shit is covered in blood, no thanks to you," I bite back.

"You sat there," he replies.

The audacity of him. I grab my dress and throw it at his head. It does nothing but cover up his cell phone. He shrugs it off, standing and sliding his cell into his pocket.

"I just can't with you."

"But you can."

"No, I really can't." I shake my head.

He reaches into the drawer and pulls out another dress, his face inches from mine as he stares at me. "I could kiss you right now."

"I wouldn't allow it," I tell him, but my eyes betray me and flick to his lips, then back to his eyes.

"But you would."

Damn him, he's not wrong.

Lucas pulls back and hands me the dress. "Put this on. The clean-up crew has arrived." Then he walks out.

Clean-up crew?

What the hell is a fucking clean-up crew?

After sliding on the dress, I walk out but quickly run back in to grab my cell from my discarded jeans pocket before I make my way down the stairs. When I reach the bottom, Lucas is speaking with Sergio and Joey. A few others are there, dressed in an all-white get-up with gloves on as they clean the house.

"You brought her here?" Joey says, gaze locked on me. All eyes fix on me at that statement, and I feel Joey's rake me over before they go back to an angry Lucas.

"Did you have to eye fuck her?" Lucas asks.

Joey just smirks. "Did you have to kill Angela?" Joey bites back.

"Yes, but did you have to eye fuck Chanel?" Lucas asks again.

"Chanel." Joey turns to face me. "She is beautiful to look at." I watch in slow motion as Lucas pulls a gun from his pants and raises it at Joey. Joey ignores him and keeps his eyes on me.

"It's probably best you leave. You shouldn't have even been here."

I nod.

A part of me wants to walk out of the house and leave Lucas there, but the other…

I walk up to Lucas slowly and place my hand on his arm, the same one that is holding the gun. "Lucas, take me home." His long eyelashes blink a few times before he lowers his weapon and turns, catching my arm and storming out of the room.

*L*ucas didn't talk the whole way back to my place. He sat in the back with me again while Sergio drove. When we pulled up, I got out, but he made sure to pass me my cell as I did, then he shut the door and drove away.

"Holy shit! That dress is everything. Let me borrow it," Merci says as I unlock the door to my house.

"Where is Brody?" I ask.

"He said he had to go to work." She follows me in, and I tear the dress over my head and pass it to her. "You can have it."

"Oh my God, really?" She immediately starts ripping her own clothes off before she slides the dress on. Then she does a spin, showing it off.

"Where is your underwear?" she asks, stopping mid-spin. I shrug and walk into my bedroom, sliding on panties and quickly getting dressed again.

"So, the boss has been asking if you're coming back." She taps her foot on the floor. "Says your clients have been annoying him."

"I work for Sailor now. I hope to never have to go back to that life," I tell her. "I make more and have to do less, and it's good, not just good money but good everything."

"Think you can get me a job?" She chuckles,

then sits on my bed. "Where have you been, I saw Lucas' car pull away."

"Someone stole it, and he had to go collect it."

"Stole it?" Her eyes go wide. "Who would be that stupid?"

"I know, right?" I don't tell her that he killed the woman who did. Or that the reason I had that dress on was because I'd been covered in half the woman's blood, or even that she's wearing that dead woman's dress.

Maybe I'm becoming too accustomed to him and his lifestyle. I didn't come from a clean one to begin with, and I know of all the bad things that happen in this life. I've seen it and sometimes have even done some of them.

"Rumors are flying."

I sit on my bed next to her.

"What do you mean?"

She looks away and touches the bottom of the dress.

"About you both."

"Lucas and me?"

"Yeah."

"What are they saying?"

"Well, you know the streets talk, they always do. It could be false, what they say."

"What are they saying, Merci?"

"That there is a reason he's so invested in you and hasn't killed you yet."

"Did they say what the reason is?"

She shakes her head. "No, but it started to sound more and more true when Brody told me he didn't actually find the job, but that the job found him. Knowing how protective you are of your brother you would go there. And…" She pauses.

"And…" I say, indicating for her to continue.

"That he has you where he wants you. But you are too blind by the way he fucks to see clearly."

"There's no doubt he is good in bed," I point out. "But I already suspected the same thing. I just don't know exactly what it is yet."

"And you're willing to find out?"

"Lucas won't let me walk away, regardless. He isn't that type of man. So, I have no other choice." I shrug.

"You always have a choice."

"Since when? Look at where we live, what we do. Who we are?"

Merci stands, walks over, and grips my face. "But look at where you are now. You aren't that little girl that your momma abandoned anymore. You are amazing, you know that."

"Sometimes, I don't feel it," I say in a small voice.

"That's just because we aren't conditioned to it. We weren't lucky enough for that. I'm thankful for my grandmother, but I didn't always have her."

I look down at my bare right foot, where a small

scar sits. You wouldn't notice if I didn't point it out, but I remember it clearly.

They were fighting. Always, always fighting. They mentioned love, but was that really a thing if it was meant to be like that? I didn't understand it. Surely, this couldn't be right.

Brody cries from the next room, and I push open the front door. I was planning on staying on the other side until they finished, but I'm hungry, and I need to use the bathroom. Plus, I need to comfort Brody.

"You useless piece of shit." Dad's angry. When isn't he, though?

"Fuck you," my mother hisses.

"You." I stop just as I walk in. Both sets of eyes fall to me. "Where have you been?" My father walks over to me. I look back to my mother to see her turn away and grab a bottle of something with brown liquid before she lights a cigarette. My father slaps my face for not focusing on him—he hates it when I disobey him. But sometimes, I have to. He just doesn't understand, or maybe he does.

"Yes." My voice is small because I am small. But I know well enough to not argue with him. He doesn't care about hitting me. He will do it, then walk over to Mama and do the same.

He hasn't hit Brody yet, maybe because he's too little.

I don't remember a time when he didn't hit me.

"Where have you been? Your brother has been crying for

the last hour, and you know you're meant to be looking after him."

I hold up the now warm bottle of milk. He grabs and throws it. I hear it crack, and I shiver.

I had to steal that money from him to be able to get it. Brody needs milk. It's why he's screaming.

"Go and look after your brother. Shut him up." I nod and walk behind my father to the kitchen and grab a bottle. It's dirty, so I rinse it under the water as Mama stands there doing nothing but smoking. When I look at the milk, there's a little bit left in the bottom, so I pick it up and pour it in, then add some water.

Just as I screw on the lid, Dad is back, the glass from the broken bottle in his hand.

"I told you to shut him up," he screams at me. "Why is he still crying?"

I hate him.

Detest him.

Loathe the fucker and her.

I hate them both.

I shouldn't hate them.

But I can't help it.

The clothes that I am wearing are second-hand, and the shoes I wear are too small and hurt my feet. I currently have blisters all over them and my toes are curling.

"John." My mama's voice rings through. I cringe as she walks over and touches his shoulder. "Let's get high."

"Woman, you're already high. You smoked all our fucking shit." Then his dark eyes fall back to me.

"Women are good for one thing…fucking. Do you hear me, kid?" I nod, having no idea what he's talking about. "And yet, your mother sucks at it."

"John, you weren't complaining last night." I glance at my mama to see her licking her lips. Then my father places the piece of glass on the counter, picks up a knife, and turns to me. He leans in real close to my ear, and I grip the bottle hard, wanting to run, but also hearing Brody scream for me.

It's never them he screams for.

It's me.

"You'll remember what I said. Women are only good for one thing," he says into my ear.

I nod.

"You'll remember." Then he drops the knife, and it falls straight into my foot. The pain makes me scream. The bottle I was clutching falls to the floor, and my father walks away, leaving me there staring at the knife sticking out of my foot.

Angrily, I wipe the tears away and pull the knife out, silently screaming as I do. Then I grab the bottle—luckily, it didn't smash—and walk into Brody's room. Giving him the bottle, he shuts up straight away. As soon as he's settled, I open his door to peek out to see where they are. My foot is throbbing, and I need to cover it because blood is soaking the floor.

I hate blood.

They are both on the floor talking, getting high, needles hanging from their arms.

Picking Brody up, I walk us out of the room and past them to the front door.

Immediately, I head off to Merci's house and knock. Her grandmother lets us in, fixes my foot, and gives me a nice new pair of shoes that fit my feet.

We stay there for two nights.

My parents never look for us once.

"*L*ucas is here," Merci says, breaking my flashback.

I get up from the bed, taking my cell, and smile back at her.

"Tell Brody I'll be back tomorrow." I offer her a small smile before I walk out to find him waiting for me. Lucas says nothing, just turns and walks out.

I follow.

Because I'm stupid like that.

Maybe I am my mother—the one person I tried hard not to be.

CHAPTER TWENTY-NINE

LUCAS

S he walks into my house behind me, and I say, "I'm going to bed, and you're coming with me."

"You honestly think you can tell me what to do? That you can control me?" She chews the inside of her cheek.

"I don't have the patience to fight with you right now." I really don't. All I want to do is bury myself deep inside of her and forget what I have to do tomorrow.

Tomorrow.

"What am I to you? Do you even know? Or is this just a control thing?" she asks.

I pause.

I can't tell her what she is.

It would destroy us both.

"You are the woman who controls my fucking

thoughts, who takes leverage in them, and doesn't want to fucking let go."

She remains silent at my outburst at first and then whispers, "You don't even know me." She shakes her head. "I don't know you." She looks away. "Why are we doing this? Will you let me walk out and away?"

"No," I state with absolutely no hesitation.

"Figured as much."

"I know that your parents mistreated you, that you raised your brother with the help of your neighbors. I know that you love pasta and ice cream. I know that I'm the only man who can make you come. That you bite the inside of your cheek when you're nervous or antsy. And most of all, you hate that you feel something when you are around me, just as I do." I turn and stalk into my room, tearing off my clothes on the way, and I sense her behind me as I kick my trousers off.

"You have a problem with control. You think you can control every aspect of your life, and you hate that you can't control me. That's why you want me so badly," she whispers, and I turn to see her looking at the floor and not at me. "You love your mother, even though you love no one else."

"I…" I pause.

Do I love her? I'm not even sure what this is.

"And that word is so foreign to you, that I have a feeling not even your mother says it." She's right. I do love my mother, but we don't tell each other. My father never said it to her either, or me. "But I don't know anything about your father. You keep that hidden."

"I need you undressed." I reach for her, but she shakes her head.

"I'm tired, Lucas. So damn tired." She leans forward, and her head rests on my chest. She takes deep breaths, breathing me in, and I pat her head, holding her to me while my fingers stroke through her hair.

"My mother did love my father, but my father…" I pause. "He loved only himself. There is no one in this world he loved more than himself." Chanel remains quiet as she listens to me. "When I started working for Keir, I saw then that he really did only love himself. He would ask me to get him things, do things for him. Because now I had more connections than him, and he didn't like that. He hated that I was becoming more powerful than him. It stressed him to no end. He left my mother, which he should have done right after I was born, because he constantly cheated on her anyway. He would come home smelling of other women, with absolutely no remorse for how that would make my mother feel."

"Does she still love him?" Chanel asks.

"No, she's learned that it wasn't her. She always thought throughout the marriage that the problem was that she couldn't keep him happy. But there is no keeping him happy, no matter what. He was and always will be *all* about him." Even as the words leave my mouth, I know them to be true.

"Do you still talk to him?"

"Yes, he is my father."

"Just because he is, doesn't mean you should." She pulls back. "Sometimes people's love is misleading. False. Broken."

"My parents didn't have your family's dynamic," I point out.

"No, my father and mother loved each other. All through their fucked-up ways and their stupid habits, I have memories of them when they were sober. They were good when they were, though it was rare to find them that way. But when they touched the drugs…" She sighs. "It was a whole different ball game."

"I'm going to shower." I pull away from her and walk into the bathroom, stripping out of my clothes and stepping into the shower.

Her family and mine are complete opposites. I still have my parents in my life, and hers are dead because they cared more about the drugs than their own children.

"You have a problem with drugs," she says, now standing on the other side of the shower door.

"Just the idiots who ingest them," I tell her.

"What if I were to tell you I did drugs? What would you think of me, then?"

I stop washing myself and look at her. "Do you?"

"That wasn't what I asked."

"I would tell you to leave this fucking house."

"Goodbye, Lucas." She walks out, and I stand there shocked.

I would have known if she did, wouldn't I?

I've seen every inch of her body, and there is no trace of track marks. She's never had that glassy-eyed look that junkies get when they're high. And I've never seen her with any drugs or drug paraphernalia.

Fuck this! Putting my head under the water, I scream, "Fuuuck!"

Immediately, I jump out of the shower and run straight out the front door, where she's already halfway down the street. *Is she fucking crazy?* She is asking me to kill her.

"Chanel," I shout after her.

She doesn't stop.

So I jog down the sidewalk to catch up with her. "Fucking stop."

She stops with a loud huff and spins toward me. When she sees me, she rolls her eyes and looks around. "Do you really not have a problem with everyone seeing your cock?" She glances at my naked body.

"No. It only plans to be buried inside of you. So, it doesn't matter who sees it, because it will only be seeing your cunt."

"What if I were to run out of the house naked?"

"I would chase you down and spank your fucking ass." She gives me another solid eye roll. "You do drugs?" I ask her.

"I have tried them, yes," she admits.

"But you don't do them any longer, correct?"

"No, I don't."

"Come back inside."

"What if I went and got high right now? Would you kick me out again?" she asks, her arms crossing over her chest.

"No. Seems I don't like that option, so I'd just tie you to the bed and let you ride it out."

"You aren't tying me to the bed ever again."

"Oh yes, I will be, and you'll enjoy it." I reach for her hand and drag her back inside, her feet moving willingly even if her mouth says otherwise.

"What are we even doing?" she whispers, asking that same question again, as the door closes behind us.

"Lord knows, but I'm going to keep on doing it." I smoothe my hands down her back, then grab her ass and lift her up. She squeals but wraps her legs around me.

"Lucas." I pause my steps, and she pulls back and strokes my face. "I don't want to like you."

"I think it's a bit late for that, wouldn't you say?" The tiniest smile pulls from those beautiful lips, and I lean in to kiss them, but she beats me to it and kisses the corner of my mouth, then slides her face into my neck.

She still has semi-control.

And she isn't planning on letting that go.

*H*ands roam my body. Sinful hands that have taken lives. Hands that have given me pleasure, then taken it away.

Lips touch my skin. Lips that set butterflies off in my stomach. Lips that utter words so cruel that I wonder how I ever had those lips anywhere near me or my body.

"Mia per sempre."

"Tell me what it means?" I ask, clutching his face in my hands. We're on the bed, and he's spent the last few minutes undressing and kissing as many parts of my body as possible.

Kisses as hot as fire.

Hands as cool as the night breeze.

Breaths tickle and linger in places, as if trying to pause a moment in time.

"It means 'forever mine,'" he says simply, then kisses my belly. His tongue dips into my belly button and I squirm at the sensation before he drops lower.

"Is that what I am to you? Yours?" He raises his head and rests his chin on my belly as he lies between my naked legs.

"You won't be anyone else's."

I reach down and touch his face, my fingers trailing through his hair and down his cheek. "We are toxic."

Lucas leans into my touch. "I'm toxic, you are not. And…" he pauses, laying his head on my stomach, "… I will kill anyone who tries to take you away from me."

"Lucas."

"Hmm."

"Why aren't you inside of me already?"

He lifts his head and climbs back up my body, then leans down and kisses my collarbone, working his way around to my chin, and making sure he kisses every part of me. His hand comes up and his thumb slides over my lips before his finger slips into my mouth.

"Suck," he commands, and I do. His eyes darken as he watches the action before he pulls it out and puts it between us and rubs my clit. I feel his cock near my entrance. Lucas rubs, and rubs a little more, and soon my legs wrap around his waist, his mouth touching my skin, setting it on fire with his lingering kisses before he gently slides into me.

How did I not know sex could be this amazing?

How did I not know that there is pure, addictive pleasure in it?

I had sex because it was my job. And sometimes I would start to become aroused, but the feeling went as fast as it came. And I fucked because I was paid to, nothing more.

I don't fuck Lucas for any of those reasons.

He is one of the first men I fucked for the pure pleasure of it and nothing more.

That's a lie. There is more, but I'm not ready to deal with that 'more' word just yet.

I shouldn't have to.

I don't *want* to.

His hand comes up to my neck, and he applies pressure. I bite my lip as he starts moving in and out.

"If you stop…" I warn him.

A soft chuckle leaves his mouth. "I couldn't even if I fucking wanted to." I can hear the desperation in his voice, and a part of me wants him to kiss me, but the other part that I'm keeping to myself—the one I don't want to let him have—is screaming at me to say no.

If I give him my all, he will break me.

Lucas is known to break women.

And most don't come back alive.

I want to continue breathing, so I keep my lips to myself and don't go down that path.

Mainly to protect myself.

Because that's all I have left.

Myself.

He has everything else. My body, my touches, my attention.

But he will not get the kisses because those are mine to give.

Lucas keeps up a perfect rhythm, and he does it ever so slowly, like he has to savor me. He's never rushed because he knows how to please. And please me he has always done.

"*Mia per sempre.*"

I grip and kiss his cheek. Then I run my fingers through his hair. He stops, and I almost want to scream, but he gets up on his knees and lifts my legs over his shoulders before he slides right back into me. Not before he leans over and grabs something —a knife.

That's when I watch him fuck me. The way his muscles clench and move, his V arrowing down to his talented cock, the lines of tattoos covering every inch of his chest.

I want to discover what each and every one of those inked images means.

Why? A quiet voice asks me.

I grip my tits, and he smirks as he watches me pinch my nipples. He picks up the pace. Not fast enough to '*slam bam thank you ma'am*,' but enough that I can feel myself on the edge. And he's right there to push me over.

"Touch your clit," he commands. I slide one of my hands from my breasts down to my clit, then I lean up and offer him my finger. He takes it and sucks before he realizes. Then he grips it and pauses while he's inside of me.

"Stay still," he commands. I watch in horror as he brings that knife down to my stomach.

"No," I immediately say. He smirks then holds out his wrist in front of me, while his cock is still in me.

"Watch," he commands. He digs the knife in, it cuts his arm open and blood begins to pool, not deep enough for blood to gush, but enough that blood is evident. He places the knife down and puts his fingers on his arm where he cut and puts the blood on his finger pushing on his skin to push more blood out, before he pulls it away and smirks as he puts it between us and onto my clit.

It's sadistic. He's a sociopath, of that I'm sure. But why, oh fuck why, does it turn me on as he rubs me with his own blood. My hips start moving and he whispers, "Don't stop." My hand wants to pull and clutch his hair. "Don't stop," he repeats.

A soft groan leaves me as my other hand squeezes my breast to the point of pain.

"That's a good girl," he says as I come, then his pace picks up and he's coming right along with me.

"You are my favorite show," he says, coming back down to put his full weight on me. My clit is sensitive, but the warmth of his body feels good over me.

"Hmm," is all I manage to get out. Not even thinking about the blood, and I really should be. I've done some fucked up things, but that tops it all.

Lucas lays his head between my breasts, and soon, we both pass out.

❧

*I*t's a normal day, as normal as any day could be, really. I come home from school to find Brody sitting on the steps. He should have been at school, he's old enough, but he hardly went anymore.

"What's wrong?" I sit next to him, nudging him with my shoulder when he doesn't speak. Sometimes he prefers to be quiet, because our father won't hit him if he is. He learned that quickly.

"I need to use the bathroom." His legs are squeezed tightly together.

"Okay, well, let's go." I stand, offering him my hand, but he shakes his head.

"I don't want to go in there. He kicked me out, and I

couldn't go to school because he wouldn't give me my backpack. The kids at school already make fun of me for what I wear," he grumbles, looking down at his bare feet.

I picked up some part-time work as soon as I was old enough, which means Brody has to spend more time at home without me.

And I hate it.

But I have to do it because we need to eat, and all our parents' money goes straight to drugs. And that's where it stays. They haven't changed over the years, and they never will. I came to accept that fact a long time ago.

"Okay, let's walk you over to Merci's. I'm sure she and her grandmother are home. You can use their bathroom while I go and get some things."

He nods and leans on me when he stands. I have to go to work in a few hours, but if Merci is home, I'm sure he'll be fine to stay there.

When we get to Merci's place, Brody knocks softly and she opens the door, smiling.

"Grandma's just cooked, perfect timing." I push him in, and he heads straight for the bathroom. We stand there for a moment before she looks back to me. "It's been quiet over there. I was wondering where he was."

"He's been on the front steps." She nods like she gets it, and she probably does. Her mother was the same, it's why she lives here.

We don't have any other family to lean on, as far as I am aware; it's only ever been us. No one else.

No one has ever come to save us.

And *I* always knew *I*'d have to do it.

"*I* have to get a few things from home. Can he stay here tonight on your couch?"

"What about you?" she asks, biting her lip nervously.

"*I*'ll be fine."

"You aren't always fine. *I* see the bruises, Chanel. *I* know they hit you."

She's right, they do. They throw things at me and laugh, thinking it's some sort of stupid game. *I*'ve gotten to that age now, though, where *I* can overpower them. The drugs have made them weak.

That's how *I* see them.

Weak, weak, parents who couldn't give a shit about anyone but themselves.

It took me a while to view them as that, but now, that's all *I* see.

Who would bring children into this world if they don't intend to do the basic things for them like feed and clothe them? Selfish assholes, that's who, and *I* have two of them.

"*I*'ll be back." She nods and watches me walk to my door. *I* push it open, because it's never locked, and *I*'m met with silence. Bongs sit on the coffee table in the living room and cigarette butts litter the floor. One time, *I* came home from school to find Brody drinking the bong water. Right then and there, *I* knew *I* could never trust them with him.

"Hello."

No one answers.

I walk farther inside and see the tap running in the kitchen. Turning it off, *I* hear a faint sound.

The apartment has only two bedrooms.

At first, Brody had their room, but now he shares a room with me. It's safer that way. If they get high during the night, I barricade us in the room.

Passing our room, I go straight to theirs and push open the door slightly.

I pause.

Well fuck! I didn't expect to see this.

I mean, I had a feeling one day it would happen, but I was hoping it would be after I was eighteen. Not before.

Stepping in, I find my father—the piece of shit that he is—eyes wide open and froth at his mouth. Clearly, he's overdosed. I lean down and check his pulse. When I feel nothing, I kick him. Asshole. The fucking asshole. "I hate you," I scream, kicking him again.

"Chanel." I jump at the sound of my mother's voice. She's on the bed, while my father is on the floor. Stepping over him, I go closer to her. She reaches out to touch me, but she's too weak and gives up. "Help." The voice she uses rocks me. A part of me wants to go and get help. While the other part...

Smack.

Useless piece of shit you are.

Smack.

I wish you were never born.

Smack.

I hate you.

Smack.

That's what I remember when I look at her—the way she is when she isn't asleep.

She's an evil bitch.

Just like that piece of shit lying dead on the floor.

"No." The word falls from my mouth, and shock shows in her eyes, but she is too weak to move or do anything. I sit on the edge of the bed next to her. "Brody and I, we are going to have such a better life without you two in it," I tell her. "You are poison, and I hate you with every fiber of my being."

"Chanel." Her voice comes out soft. "What about Brody?" And that's the card she will always play with me—my little brother.

"No one will know. I'm eighteen soon, then I'll report you." I stand and lean down over her. My hand shakes as I reach it out and touch her face, gripping her nose and covering her mouth with my palm. She's too weak to fight me. "Burn in hell, Mother. I'll see you real soon." I hold on tight. She struggles, but not too much as the drugs having taken a toll on her. I watch as she tries to catch her last breath and happiness fills me when she can't.

What does this make me?

A killer?

When she stops moving, I remove my hand and check her pulse.

Dead.

Good.

Stepping over my father, I turn and walk out of the

room, *shutting the door and locking it so Brody won't go in and find them.*

Then a smile touches my face.

It's done.

They are done.

All the pain and suffering...

... it's over.

CHAPTER THIRTY-ONE
CHANEL

"*C*hanel." Hands grab me. I try to move, but Lucas keeps me still. "Chanel," he says my name again, and when I open my eyes, I'm not stuck in that shitty apartment I called home with my dead parents.

"Sorry, bad dream." I rub my eyes.

"You have them often?" he asks in a softer voice.

"Who are you?" I ask him. "You aren't the man you made yourself out to be," I say without thinking, the strange comfort I feel in his arms making me want to understand him even more. I can't imagine him killing me now, or that he would actually harm me.

I could be wrong, but I hope I'm not.

"And what type of man is that?" he questions,

his hand tightening on my bare hip as he keeps me pinned to him.

"They call you the viper. They say you collect. Have you collected me yet?" I ask.

"Do you think I haven't?"

I think on that for a second.

Has he? He has, but I think I like the way he did it.

"Maybe you have."

"I have." He strokes the hair away from my face.

I go to get up, but he holds me still. "I have work today."

"Call in sick." He plays with a piece of my hair, twirling it around his finger.

"I only just got this job. I need it."

"I'll call in sick for you. Tell Sailor I need your assistance today."

"No, don't." I shake my head and try to get up again, but he just pulls me right back down.

"Okay, how much longer do we have, then?"

I roll over and check the time. "I have to leave in an hour," I reply, turning back to him.

"I can deal with an hour." He pulls the duvet up over us and then scoots down and pushes my legs apart. I go to stop him, because of what we did, but when I look to the side there's a wash cloth covered in blood and I realize he cleaned me while I slept. His mouth doesn't waste a second before it lands between my legs. I groan as I slide farther into him and reach under the blanket to grip his hair. His hand snakes up my body, finding my breast before he grips my nipple, squeezing and tugging it.

"Lucas."

"Hmm," he hums into me.

"Someone is at your door," I tell him, hearing the faint knocking.

He doesn't stop. In fact, he doesn't seem to care at all that someone is here.

I giggle as he slaps my nipple, then moves his hand back down to slide his finger into me.

"No giggling," he commands, and that automatically brings up another giggle, until his mouth does that thing where it licks with his whole tongue, incredibly slowly over my clit. Then I shut up and moan. "That's better," he says, then continues with what he's doing. My head lolls back on the pillow, and I can't help but call out his name as he makes me come.

The knocking grows louder, but my moans drown them out.

"Chanel."

"Hmm," is all I can manage as he spreads my legs and puts himself between them.

"You weren't mine. Did you know that?"

I don't know what to say to that, so I keep my mouth shut, my eyes asking all he needs to respond.

"You were his."

This makes my eyes open wider. "What?"

He pauses inside of me and leans forward, his mouth hovering before he leans down and kisses my chin and then bites my ear. "But I think I may keep you. Maybe." A soft groan leaves him as he pushes all the way in. I dig my nails into his back as he takes me, and I let him because he knows what he's doing.

Lucas is a good lover. No, Lucas is a marvelous lover.

No man I have ever been with has fucked me the way Lucas does.

And that's saying a lot considering I've slept with my fair share of men.

"Tell me it's me you want," he says, pushing in and stopping. He gazes down at me, and I reach up to push some of his hair away from his face.

I hate that this man, who is so evil, is so damn beautiful.

He can fool the best of them.

When God created Lucas, he said, *I'm going to make you so fine, that women will drop at your feet.*

Literally.

Dead.

And Lucas said, *Challenge accepted, bitch.*

Well, in my head that's how it went.

The knocking continues.

Lucas is still waiting for my words.

"It's you," I whisper, which makes a small, sinister smile touch his lips before he starts moving again. He leans down, and this time when he comes to my lips, I let him. He halts, as if he isn't sure. He's giving me time to push him away, to tell him no.

"Lucas."

He freezes, and so do I.

The knocking has stopped, and now that person is in the house.

Lucas pulls out of me, throws the duvet over me, picks up a pair of pants and slides them on, then looks back at me. "Do *not* move. Stay in this room."

I nod as he looks me in the eyes one last time.

"You'll forgive me." Then he walks out.

What is that supposed to mean?

I stay there, frozen in shock until I hear talking. So I decide to get up and get ready for the day since I don't plan on missing work. Lucas mentioned earlier he's had some clothes brought over and they're in a bag in the closet. I find the bag and open it. The outfit is long work pants with a silky black singlet. After getting dressed, I go to his bathroom and fix my hair. Once it's styled enough, I walk back into the bedroom to find Lucas sitting on the bed, with the door open.

"Plans have changed," he states, standing and

walking to his closet. He gets dressed, and I watch him, confused by his words. When he turns back to me, he's doing up his buttons. "You should leave."

"Okay." I reach for my cell and walk out of his bedroom with a little bit of anger, pain and rejection hitting me at his words. I stop short at the sight before me blocking the front door.

"Hello, Chanel. That's your real name, correct?" My eyes go wide, and I clutch the cell in my hand. "I mean, I didn't really think Mandy was your name, so it was harder to find you." I step back as he steps up to me.

I bump into something and am relieved to feel it's Lucas. His hands come up to my arms and he grips them.

"Chanel, meet my father, Malik."

A small gasp leaves me.

This man is not his father, he can't be.

I had him as a client.

He kept on requesting me, and eventually I had to put a stop to it. He became weird and made me uncomfortable, so I put a restraining order on him when he started demanding I leave with him and be his.

I didn't want to do that, so I did what I had to.

"I need to leave," I say, the words barely leaving me as I try to step back.

"That's not going to happen anytime soon," Malik responds clicking his tongue.

"You shouldn't be near me," I tell him.

"You are in my son's house. It was you who came here."

I go to move, but Lucas holds me still.

"You are still so beautiful. Tell me, have you missed me?"

"No," I hiss at him. "I never even liked you, but somehow you never really understood that."

"But you like my son. Is it the age difference?" he asks.

"No, it's your personality. It is fucked."

He throws his head back and laughs. "That's funny, considering I just walked in on you fucking my son for free. And he is just like me."

"No, he isn't."

Lucas lifts a hand and strokes my face from behind me. "But I am. Where do you think I learned everything?"

A cold, calculated shiver runs down my spine.

"I need to go."

"Sailor isn't expecting you today, Chanel. I've already messaged her." I try to check my cell, but Malik snatches it from my hand and tosses it aside.

Lucas lets me go and steps around me until he's standing next to Malik.

When I look at them standing side by side, I see it. The way they look like father and son. Malik isn't a bad-looking man, but he is fucked-up. I guess just like Lucas. So why was I attracted to him, then?

"Was this the plan from the beginning?" I ask Lucas.

He steps forward so he is closer to me. "You didn't really think I hired your brother because I needed help, did you? I have enough help, you should know that. I hired him because of what I'd learned about you prior, and that was that you protect him. So much so, that I knew you would burst in when I was there. Granted, it took you a few days, but you eventually came. And when you did, my cock was fucking hard. You were just so perfect, so beautiful, that I had to have a taste before I gave you to him."

I glance at his father. "You made your son come after me?"

"I always get what's mine, and you are mine."

I look back to Lucas who's grinding his teeth.

He doesn't like hearing that.

Why, though, when he was so willing to give me up just seconds ago?

"I'm no one's, especially not yours, old man."

Malik steps forward, and his hand lifts and then slaps me hard across my cheek, snapping my head to the left. "Watch your words, whore."

"Oh, you don't like to be called... *old man*. You don't like the fact you're aging and have to pay to fuck women?"

"I pay to fuck women so I can do what I want."

He smiles. "It's why we would be perfect together. You're a whore, and you liked it when I fucked you."

"Wrong. I never came…not once. It was all fake." I smile through the sting in my cheek, and the ache in my chest. "The only person who has ever made me come is your son."

Malik slaps me again, then he punches me in my stomach so hard, I fall over. I manage to catch my breath and see both of them looking down at me.

"I would advise you to shut up."

"Not going as you had planned, Daddy? That you aren't all you thought you are and that your sperm…" I pause and nod to Lucas, who has a face on him that looks like he would take death gladly, "… fucks me better then you?"

"I know what you're doing." Malik drops down until he is face-to-face with me. "I know you killed your mother, that you left their bodies in your apartment to rot until you reached the right age. Brody will be fine. Lucas will take him on. You, though…you are all mine." Malik reaches for me, but I kick him in the shin, which makes his hand on my arm drop.

"Stop it." We both turn to look at Lucas as his eyes fall to me. "You were never mine. I just borrowed you," he states, his tone cold like when I first met him, then he looks to his father. "Take her and hurry the fuck up about it. I have work to do." He walks off, leaving me in his living room with his arrogant asshole of a father.

"Looks like not even my son wants you. Don't you see? We are perfect together."

"You're a sick fuck. You had a wife, a child, a life. And what did you have after? Whores, as you like to say. Because you fuck like a ninety-year-old man and look like one too. I'd rather fuck your son again, at least he knows how to make a woman come," I scream at him. How could Lucas betray me like this. That's right, he is Lucas. I should have expected it really.

I know what I did.

I practically asked for it.

But did you really think I was going to go down without a fight? No fucking way.

I don't have my knife on me, and I'm so fucking mad I don't. But when his hand comes down fast and hard to my face my last thought is…

… payback will be a bitch.

And after this man is done, I'm going after Lucas.

Because I *will* survive.

My parents doubted me and look where that got them.

It's wrong for others to doubt me as well.

I will do whatever is necessary to save Brody and myself.

No matter the cost.

No matter the life.

The last thing I hear is Lucas' footsteps, and I wonder…

Was it all a game to him?

The City's Bad Boy

It's been mentioned that the city's bad boy has been seen
without his mystery woman.
I wonder what that means.
Did he move on and find someone else?
Will she be found at the bottom of a river, like one of his last
known lovers?
So many questions.
And we need all the answers…

FIRST CHAPTER OF
UNL I KE LY QUEEN

The prophecy foretold of the true queen...

In the new world, where the old world is long forgotten, an evil queen sits on the throne, and anyone who challenges her reign is a mortal enemy —I am that enemy just by breathing.

The queen always gets what she wants, and she wants me dead.

Then one day, my life is turned upside down by a prophecy naming me the one true queen. I was oblivious to the true roles of the two men in my life—the Angel of Light and the Angel of Death—as my existence hung in the balance. One man there to save me, the other to claim me should the queen succeed in her quest for my blood.

But every time she nearly succeeds in my demise, my dark angel swoops in, pulling me back to safety. Making the world stop. Pulling everything back in balance.

Tired of being hunted by the vampires, slaves to the queen, I decide to fight back. It's the only way to survive. I'm going to tear down the wards one by one and free my allies—the witches and the wolves—and then I'm going to force the queen from the safety of her castle and claim what's rightfully mine.

Her kingdom.

Her throne.

Her crown.

Available February 2022

ABOUT THE AUTHOR

USA Today Best Selling Author T.L. Smith loves to write her characters with flaws so beautiful and dark you can't turn away. Her books have been translated into several languages. If you don't catch up with her in her home state of Queensland, Australia you can usually find her travelling the world, either sitting on a beach in Bali or exploring Alcatraz in San Francisco or walking the streets of New York.

facebook.com/authortlsmith

instagram.com/tlsmith1313

goodreads.com/T_L_Smith

bookbub.com/authors/t-l-smith

ALSO BY T. L. SMITH

Kandiland

Pure Punishment (Standalone)

Antagonize Me (Standalone)

Degrade (Flawed #1)

Twisted (Flawed #2)

Black (Black #1)

Red (Black #2)

White (Black #3)

Green (Black #4)

Distrust (Smirnov Bratva #1) FREE

Disbelief (Smirnov Bratva #2)

Defiance (Smirnov Bratva #3)

Dismissed (Smirnov Bratva #4)

Lovesick (Standalone)

Lotus (Standalone)

Savage Collision (A Savage Love Duet book 1)

Savage Reckoning (A Savage Love Duet book 2)

Buried in Lies

Distorted Love (Dark Intentions Duet 1)

Connect with T.L Smith by tlsmithauthor.com

Printed in Great Britain
by Amazon

10655427R00167